CROCODILE RIVER

Geoffrey Malone spent most of his childhood in Africa, where he managed to avoid any formal education until the age of eleven. After school in England, he spent sixteen years in the army, mis-reading maps in the Far East, Persian Gulf and Europe. He later joined a Canadian public relations agency and worked and travelled extensively in North America, becoming a regular broadcaster. His first book, *Brunner*, was inspired by a family of beavers who were his nearest neighbours while living in a remote part of Ontario. He has two sons and now lives happily in London with his wife and a spaniel, Harriet.

CROCODILE RIVER

GEOFFREY MALONE

Hodder
Children's
Books

A division of Hodder Headline Limited

A Catalogue record for this book is available from
the British Library.

ISBN 0340 77326 X

Typeset by Avon Dataset Ltd, Bidford-on-Avon, Warks

Printed and bound in Great Britain by
Clays Ltd, St Ives plc

Hodder Children's Books
A Division of Hodder Headline Limited
338 Euston Road
London NW1 3BH

To Sally Graves, my mother-in-law,
with love.

Foreword

Kyrek watched the flock of wild goats pick its way between the anthills. He lay very still, sinking the great weight of his body down below the surface of the river until only the top of his nostrils and his eyes showed. His tail moved very slightly to counter the current that was urging him downstream towards the sea. He could feel it pushing against his jaws.

He had heard the goats coming from some distance away when it had still been starlight. The noise of their hooves echoed across the hard-packed earth and down into the water where Kyrek lurked. The crocodile recognized the sounds immediately and knew the goats were coming to drink. They would come to the same place on the river bank just as they had done for the past two mornings. They were creatures of habit like all warm-blooded animals. Kyrek's eyes gleamed.

He moved his massive head to one side, assessing their progress and with a delicate paddle of his rear legs, moved out towards the middle of the river. Behind him, the sun had cleared the horizon and was gathering itself to leap up into the sky.

Already, the land was flooded with brilliant light. Twenty miles to the north, it fingered the tops of the mangrove swamps that fringed the great gulf. Ten miles wide, the mangroves formed an impenetrable barrier of twisted roots and stinking grey mud.

It was a world made only for the creatures that hunted or hid in its gloom. And for countless millions of mosquitoes. It was also the only part of the whole continent untroubled by the pitiless glare of the sun.

Across the stony plains and deserts, lizards came out of their holes to greet the new day. They stood motionless, basking in the warmth of the sun. Their thin black tongues flicking in and out, absorbing information on the air all round them. By midday, they would hide under boulders to stop their blood boiling.

As the sun's rays grew stronger, so the appearance of the land began to change. The low range of hills beyond the river flared into glowing bands of orange, brown and purple rock. In an instant, the shadows melted away into the deepest crevices bringing the outcrops into three-dimensional life.

There was a pause in Creation, a moment of anticipation while the coolness of the night fought a last battle and failed, as it always did. The noise of jet engines high overhead was absorbed in the immensity of the dawn. A warm breeze began to stir, ruffling the surface of the river where Kyrek lay in wait.

The flock was led by an old male with curling horns and a grey beard that straggled under his chin. He was thirsty and impatient to drink. Kyrek could hear him bleating bad-temperedly, chiding the others towards the river.

There were six of them, just as there had been yesterday and the day before. For a moment they milled around, waiting for the old male to assert his authority and lead them to drink.

The billy goat trotted towards the bank where he stopped and looked around. He cocked his head and listened. Reassured, he gave a bleat and jumped

3

down on to the damp sand at the water's edge. The rest followed him one by one.

With an imperceptible sweep of his tail, Kyrek eased forward. Two more careful thrusts and he was gliding across the twenty metres that separated him from the little flock. The faintest of ripples spread out on either side of his jaws but Kyrek knew they would not be seen. The glare off the water was shining straight into the goats' eyes. He had already taken that into account. The goats straddled their forelegs in the water and dipped their heads down to drink.

Kyrek had marked his prey, a well-developed kid who was the last to drink. He had been head-butting and tussling with his brother, mimicking the behaviour of rutting males. Ten metres away, the crocodile watched the little hooves skittering across the red sand. And then abruptly, the kid stopped its play and looked at the river. Kyrek measured the spot where he knew it would stoop to drink. With infinite care he drifted closer. He was very near now, the energy for the attack building inside him.

The kid lowered its muzzle. As it did so, Kyrek saw the old male flinch and throw up his head in alarm. For a split second, crocodile and goat stared

4

at one another. Then Kyrek swung his tail in a powerful heave, dug down with his back legs and with jaws gaping came up out of the river in one terrible fluid movement.

For an instant, the great crocodile hung over the little goat. Then, seizing it by the head, Kyrek fell back in a sheet of water, rolling over as he did so on top of the goat, crushing the air from its lungs. A moment later, they both sank from view.

The rest of the flock fled in panic, barging into one another, frantic to get away from that dreadful place. They raced helter-skelter under the thorn trees and away into the surrounding bush. The river boiled and seethed for a couple more minutes then settled down again and the day got under way.

One

'This your first time in Australia?' the air stewardess asked.

Tom Woods nodded and grinned up at her. He was a stocky, tousle-haired boy of about fourteen with serious eyes and a friendly smile.

'So how long you over for?' the woman questioned.

'Three weeks!' Tom told her. 'School holidays,' he explained.

The stewardess looked impressed. 'All right for some,' she said. 'Like a packet of peanuts or a drink?' She indicated the trolley she was pushing.

The flight from Heathrow had taken over sixteen hours. Tom felt grubby and cramped. He had also never drunk so much cola in all his life. He started to shake his head but then on impulse changed his mind. 'Well, just one more, please,' he asked, a little shyly.

The stewardess, whose name was Abigail, pushed back a strand of loose hair and laughed. 'Sounds familiar! So who you staying with?'

'My aunt and uncle. Bob and Sarah Bradley,' Tom told her, taking the plastic beaker. 'They live near Darwin. On a cattle ranch. I'm going to help with the round-up,' he added, watching to see her reaction.

She looked interested. 'Well, just keep your wits about you. Cattle up there are pretty wild. Easy to get hurt.'

'My father's a vet,' he replied.

'That's fine then,' she said. 'You'll know all about it.'

'Well . . .' he began. Then blushed, thinking of the cramped surgery and tiny waiting room where people from the nearby estate brought their cats and budgerigars for treatment. 'Well . . . not that much.'

But she was already busy with the people in the row behind. He looked at his watch and wondered what time it was back home. His parents had both thought he'd been joking when he had told them that he was saving to go to Australia.

'I'm sure your Uncle Bob would love to see you,' said his father, 'but . . .'

'It's far too far away and besides, we can't afford it!' his mother interrupted.

But Tom had taken a job after school and at weekends. And that was a year ago. When he told them at Christmas just how much he had saved, they were amazed. They all sat down at the kitchen table and helped Tom write a letter to his aunt and uncle. The reply came back two weeks later. 'Come for as long as you like. Hope you like hard work!'

After that, life became very hectic. Tom had been flat out, what with school assessments and the job. But it was worth it! The flight alone was magic. Nobody at school had ever done a trip as long as this! Not even Seymour, whose family came from Tobago. That was only a seven hour trip.

He gazed out of the window marvelling at the huge emptiness of Australia. There were no roads, no railway lines, no canals, no towns not even a village anywhere. Just parched red land that stretched unbroken to the far horizon.

He must have dozed off because when he woke

the plane was banking steeply and the pilot was telling them that they'd be on the ground in Darwin in twelve minutes. At the airport, he had his first disappointment. There was no one there to meet him. For the next quarter of an hour he watched the arrivals hall empty and was just going up to the information desk, when a voice behind him said, 'Tom Woods.'

It was a statement of fact not a question. He turned and saw a strongly-built boy of about fifteen standing looking at him. He was what his mother would have called 'a strapping lad'. He was a good head taller than Tom and wore a sweat-stained T-shirt which had 'Do It In Darwin' printed across the front. He was in shorts and workboots. His face was familiar.

'Gregory!' Tom exclaimed, mentally placing him from the photograph they had been sent. He had been expecting his aunt or uncle to meet him. Probably both. His shoulder bag slipped down his arm. A magazine fell out.

'Hi there! Hello!' he began, then gasped as his cousin's hand crushed his in a powerful grip.

Tom bent down hurriedly and stuffed the magazine back into the bag. It kept sticking halfway down. 'I was getting worried,' he joked a little breathlessly, getting quickly back to his feet. 'In case I'd got the wrong day or something.'

His cousin moved the gum he was chewing to the other side of his mouth. 'The name's Greg. And we're out the back.' He jerked a thumb towards the glass exit doors. 'Better get a trolley. It's a bit of a way to the car park.'

'How did you know it was me?' Tom asked a moment later, pushing his luggage trolley after him.

'You look like a Pom,' Greg said matter-of-factly, heading towards a car park. 'All grey and pasty.'

Tom blinked in surprise and stared at Greg's back. He decided it was the sort of thing Greg probably would say and shrugged. One of the wheels on the trolley jammed as soon as they got outside. Tom wrestled it round a corner.

Greg walked quickly, keen to get going. 'I'm a bit late because I had to see the girlfriend,' he said casually. 'Know much about horses? Do you ride?'

'Only buses,' Tom joked, then wished he hadn't. It sounded silly. 'We live in the middle of a city,' he explained. 'It's just houses and things.'

Greg didn't seem to have heard. He indicated a battered red pick-up truck and went round to the driver's door. 'Stow your kit in the back,' he ordered and watched as a perspiring Tom heaved his two suitcases up over the side.

'Where the others?' Tom asked.

'Like who?'

'Well, your mum and dad.'

'They're around,' Greg said casually. 'Hop in!'

'You're not going to drive, are you!' Tom asked in astonishment.

'Sure! Why not?'

'Wow! I mean . . . fantastic! I didn't think you'd be old enough. That's all.'

Greg started the engine. 'We're a bit more practical out here,' he said slowly. 'If you live where we do, everyone drives. They have to.'

'I wasn't being rude or anything,' Tom explained as they backed out of the parking space. 'Just surprised, that's all.'

Greg did not reply.

They drove in silence. Tom felt at a loss. The inside of the truck was coated with a film of red dust. There was orange peel on the floor under his feet. He racked his brains for something to say.

'Do you like football?' he asked suddenly.

'Some,' Greg nodded.

'I mean United and Arsenal . . .'

Greg turned his head and looked at him. 'You don't mean soccer, do you?'

Tom smiled weakly.

'Bunch of overpaid softies,' Greg told him. 'I thought you meant American football.'

'Oh yes! That's good too!'

Greg's face became animated. 'Great game. Not as good as Aussie Rules though. You watch much of that?'

Tom thought quickly. 'They had bits of the final on TV. It looked brilliant,' he added. 'How are your parents? I'm really looking forward to meeting them.'

'Mum's fine,' Greg said. 'She'll be busy right now on the radio set talking to Dad and the neighbours.' He looked over at Tom. 'You haven't forgotten?' he questioned. 'We told you in the last letter. It's the cattle muster. Always happens this time of year. You'll see when you get out there. Dad always calls in about now if there's anything they need at camp. If it's urgent, he flies the chopper back to pick it up. If it's too big, I bring it up in this. Anyway, he's coming back this evening to meet you.'

'You've got a helicopter!'

Greg gave a slight grin. 'Yeah. Everyone has this time of year. We rent it. Saves weeks rounding up the cattle.'

Tom digested this information, remembering his own family's battered Renault while they drove through the wide, clean streets of Darwin. It was like being in a film, he thought. At any moment the director would shout 'Cut!' and the sky would turn grey and British double-decker buses would swish past in the rain. Instead, a flock of budgerigars flashed in front of them and swooped into the branches of a tree.

'You've got a great tan,' Tom said a little later as they drove along a wide straight road bordered by shady gum trees, 'do you go surfing much? I saw some great beaches just before we landed.'

Greg looked over at him and moved his chewing gum around. 'Don't get much chance,' he said.

'I thought everybody swam in Australia.'

'Depends,' Greg shrugged. 'There's not much swimming where we are. The rivers get pretty big in the Wet when the rains come, but then you've got crocodiles to look out for.'

'Why don't you go to the beaches?' Tom asked, puzzled.

'We would if we could,' Greg said. 'There's only one slight snag.'

'What's that?'

'Nearest one's two hundred miles away.'

Tom sat up. 'But the address you gave us said Darwin,' he protested.

Greg looked amused. 'Sure. But it's a post box number. They deliver weekly whenever they can or we pick it up if we're in town.'

'So how far are we going?'

Greg laughed. 'There's a turn-off a bit further on,' he said. 'Just wait and see.'

He was still chuckling as they drove off the metalled highway on to a dirt road where the solitary sign said, 'Balgarri 150 miles'.

Two

At the same time in the research station fifty miles beyond Balgarri, a telephone rang. 'Call for you Mr Dorrell,' a voice said.

'Who is it?' the man in the white coat demanded. 'If it's Danny or Coyle tell them I'll call 'em back.'

'Don't know who it is. Says he's got some stuff for us. You'd better take it.'

There was a pause. Then at the other end of the phone, a man cleared his throat and asked 'You the guy who wants all these rabbits delivered?' He sounded truculent. Dorrell guessed he had been drinking.

'How many have you got?' he asked.

'About five hundred I guess. Give or take a few. Say, is this some sort of joke, or what?'

'No joke, mate,' Dorrell replied, hitching the laboratory coat higher up over his shoulders. 'Our usual supplier's let us down. When can you deliver?' Dorrell could hear the man talking to someone in the background.

'Tomorrow. That suit?'

Dorrell nodded, pleased with the news. 'Great! Like to make it a regular order? Same day every week?'

The other's voice became more friendly. 'Yeah. All right. But it won't be cheap. There's a lot of work involved. It's not as easy as folks think, catching rabbits.'

Dorrell cut in. 'I'll give you the same terms for every load. Cash on delivery. Now you're sure you know how to get here?' They talked a little longer about the exact location and the right CB frequency to use. Then Dorrell rang off.

At the other end, the man stared at the telephone and began to grin. These people were crazy. All this dough for a load of rabbits! He walked over to a battered grey van and pulled open the back doors. Inside, there were rows of cages stacked up to the roof. His nose wrinkled. He had never seen so many rabbits before. It made him feel uncomfortable. And the smell! Some must have already died in the crush.

He slammed the doors tight and went round to the cab. He laid a map on the passenger seat. This was going to be the easiest money he had ever made. The thought cheered him.

He checked to make sure his knife was in its usual place and started up. He waved to a man in the shadows and drove out of the bay. He switched the radio on and reached for a can of beer. Life he thought, was sometimes really good.

Three

Greg was enjoying himself. He reckoned he had handled things pretty well. Staying a bit aloof yet appearing totally knowledgeable about everything he had been asked. But, grief! The British kid never stopped asking questions.

There was a thick clump of eucalyptus trees ahead of them and he knew they were almost home. Less than a mile to go. The dogs would have heard them coming. They'd be tearing towards them by now barking in excitement. The sun was sinking and shadows were gathering under the hills.

'Sam's due back in a couple of days,' he said suddenly. 'He's taking us out to the muster in his truck.'

'Who's Sam?' Tom asked.

'Dad's mechanic. Fixes all the vehicles,' Greg told him. 'Anything you want to know about the bush, ask him. His real name's Sam Minamurra.'

Tom looked puzzled so Greg elaborated.

'Aborigine. He can live in the middle of the desert and still survive. And when it comes to tracking,' he whistled in admiration, 'he can follow a month-old trail like you and me can read a book. You'll see.'

'How do you mean?' Tom asked.

Greg spat out of the window. 'Well,' he said deliberately. 'Let's put it this way. If you shape up OK and pull your weight like a proper Aussie at the muster, then Sam and me'll take you walkabout when the cattle are sorted.'

Then he gave a sudden whoop and slapped his hand against the outside of the door. 'Here they come!' he shouted. 'Look!' A pack of dogs appeared from nowhere, barking and racing towards them. Soon they were alongside, snapping at the wheels.

They stopped on top of a low hill. Below them was an oasis of green. There were lawns and flower beds and shady trees. Water sprinklers sent miniature rainbows high into the sky. There were white painted barns and in the middle of it all, a comfortable-looking farmhouse with flower baskets hanging in the porch.

'There she is. End of the line. Home sweet home,' Greg said with pride. They drove down into a paved yard. A man and woman were waiting for them. A large hand gripped Tom's. 'Hello there Tom! I'm Bob Bradley and this is your Aunt Sarah. Welcome to Balgarri Downs!'

Four

'Did you sleep well?' Sarah Bradley asked. 'Here. Try some pawpaw.'

Tom looked at the bright orange fruit. He had never eaten pawpaw before but he had seen them in the supermarket at home. Cautiously, he took his first mouthful. It was sweet and slippery. Greg was already on his second helping of rice krispies.

Life here was totally different. Everything was so much bigger for a start, from the huge refrigerator in the kitchen to the size of the rooms. Every bedroom had its own bath or shower. Tom thought of the solitary, cramped bathroom at home with its heated towel rail that burnt your bottom whenever you bent to dry your toes. Whatever the time of year, the window always misted up.

Although Sarah Bradley was his mother's elder sister, Tom could find very little similarity between the two of them. Sarah seemed to be able to do ten things at once without any fuss.

She was in charge of feeding the ten stockmen the station employed to look after the cattle. She also ran the farmhouse, or homestead, as they called it. Every week, she drove a hundred miles to the nearest store in the small town of Roper. She also helped out with the Flying Doctor service when needed. She was a qualified nurse. She was so totally in control that Tom was in awe of her.

Bob, his uncle, was a beefy man with heavy black eyebrows and a strong jaw. He flew back and forth in the helicopter with Jacko, the foreman and senior rider. Together, they checked and re-checked lists of stores and made numerous telephone calls. There were rolls of barbed wire, piles of sacking and wooden posts; huge tins of baked beans, processed cheese and fruit salad. They were all neatly stacked in a barn waiting to be taken out to the camp. Tom helped Sarah fill the medicine chest with bandages, splints and small bottles of snake serum.

Tom liked Jacko on sight. He was tall, very thin and a natural horseman. He was weather-beaten and his face was deeply lined. He had been with the Bradleys for five years. He was twenty-two years of age.

'Greg says you can't ride!' he said in disbelief the first time they met. 'No worries. We'll soon fix that!' But Tom did not enjoy being in the saddle. The horses immediately sensed his unease and played him up. It was a long way to fall on to ground as hard as concrete.

Then Bob discovered Tom couldn't drive either. 'Don't they teach you anything useful where you come from?' he boomed. 'There's an old crate in the back barn. Greg'll get it out for you. You can learn on that 'till Sam gets here. Keep you out of mischief.'

To his delight, Tom found driving easy. On his first morning, he got up into top gear and by the end of the day, was reversing confidently through barn doors.

Greg helped make an obstacle course using old tyres and boxes. They had just finished going round when they heard the faint sound of a horn. Tom wiped the sweat from his face and listened to the honking getting louder.

'Who's that?' he asked.

'You'll see,' replied Greg with a grin.

Sarah came out to join them. 'That'll be Sam,' she said. 'He's really looking forward to meeting you,' she told Tom.

As she finished speaking, a 4×4 truck rattled into the yard. It headed straight for the drinking trough, braking at the last possible moment. A man leapt out and plunged his head and shoulders into the water. He came up with a loud yell of relief. Then he dipped a battered old trilby into the trough and poured water over his chest and down his back.

He gave another whoop, shook himself, wiped his hands on the seat of his pants and came towards them. He was not much taller than Tom but very wiry. He had a shock of grizzled hair and markings on his forehead.

He wore a red shirt and a faded pair of jeans. He walked with a limp. Sarah put her arm around Tom and introduced the two of them. Tom felt his hand being pumped up and down. He grinned back. Sam began to speak in a language Tom had never heard before. Sam bowed his head and put a hand on his heart.

'He's welcoming you here on behalf of his ancestors and his family,' Sarah explained.

Tom managed to mumble something poli' reply.

'How's it going out there Sam?' Sarah asked.

Sam beamed round at them all. 'Great! Everything's ready. Jacko and the boys are fine.' He grinned at Tom and put a hand on his shoulder. 'Everyone's waiting for this man to come. Bob says to bring him back real quick.'

'We'll grab some food first,' Sarah told him. 'Then he's all yours.'

'How old is Sam?' Tom asked her as they went back into the kitchen.

'Search me,' replied his aunt. 'But he's been around for a long time. He's a grandfather for sure.'

They loaded Sam's vehicle with a dozen jerricans of water and covered them with a tarpaulin. Then Tom and Greg squeezed along the front seat beside Sam. Tom's heart was thumping. He had no idea what was waiting out there for him. But there was no turning back now. This was it!

They heard a shout. Sarah Bradley was running towards them holding a plastic carrier bag. 'Almost forgot to give you this,' she laughed, thrusting the bag through the window.

'For me? What is it?' asked Tom.

'Just about the most important thing in the world! Especially where you're going. Loo paper! Never be without it!'

Sam laughed until the tears trickled down his cheeks. His foot slipped off the clutch and the 4×4 kangarooed its way out of the yard. He was still chuckling long after Balgarri had disappeared from view.

Five

In a windowless laboratory in the research station, the air-conditioning hummed quietly. Dorrell squinted into the glare of the overhead lights and watched a spray of liquid shoot up from the hypodermic syringe he was holding. A row of glistening drops landed on his rubber gloves.

He gave a grunt of satisfaction and made his way down the aisle to a cage at the far end. A rabbit looked out at him with dull, incurious eyes. Dorrell put the syringe down, reached inside and dragged it towards him.

He was not a cruel man but he had a job to do. Feelings of shame were a luxury he could not afford. He searched for the exact spot just below the ear. The animal flinched and began to struggle. But he was anticipating that. Carefully, he pressed the plunger down and waited a good five seconds before pulling it out. Then he closed the door and carefully locked it.

He bent towards the cage watching intently. For a while nothing happened. The rabbit rubbed its face and then started to clean its whiskers. Suddenly, it sat bolt upright. Dorrell looked at his watch and waited.

The rabbit began to pant. Its mouth fell open. It started shivering. The shivers quickly became spasms. It got to its feet and staggered forward, bumping against the side of the cage and shaking its head in bewilderment.

The next moment, it was tearing round inside the cage, biting at its back legs, its eyes bulging. Its coat was suddenly black with sweat. The rabbit began to scream. A thin wail that froze the other animals in their cages. Flecks of foam appeared at the corners of its mouth. The rabbit flung itself in a frenzy against the wire mesh of the door and for an instant looked straight up at the man. Then it collapsed, shook convulsively and lay rigid.

Dorrell made an entry on a clipboard hanging beside the door. Then he went back to his work bench and turned a radio on. Music blared. He picked up a post-mortem knife and two kidney bowls. A disc jockey read out a commercial for a new restaurant in Darwin.

He sighed and looked at his watch. Coyle, the big boss and Danny, his side kick, would already be relaxing up there. He had watched them drive off just after breakfast. Coyle with a huge cigar stuck in his mouth.

Dorrell felt a familiar surge of resentment. He was the brains of this operation for pete's sake! Yet here he was as usual doing all the work. It had been the same ever since the syndicate had first approached him at university, three years ago.

By now, he must have made them millions! Coyle had as good as told him so late one night after too much brandy. The next morning though, he had denied ever saying it and had threatened to break Dorrell's legs if he ever repeated it.

Dorrell looked at his watch again and sighed. He was their man. They owned him. There was no way out now. Still, he consoled himself, he'd be heading up to Darwin himself in a couple more hours. He'd do his weekend shopping and have a relaxing beer or two. One of the guards would go with him of

course, just to make sure he came back. That was
also part of the deal.

Six

Kyrek lay in the warm shallows. The sun beat down through the branches mottling the river bed with shadows. He looked out from under a giant lily pad, the blazing yellow of his eyes hidden in the gloom. It was a perfect place to watch from.

Above him, a tiny red hummingbird dipped its long tongue into the flower at the centre of the pad. The beat of its wings creating a vibration which told Kyrek that the bird was too small to bother with.

A flock of parrots dipped low over the river. They screamed at one another in excitement. They were heading back to gorge themselves on a fruit tree they had discovered earlier in the day.

Kyrek followed their noisy flight with eyes that

missed nothing. He noted the height they flew over the surface and the way they crash-landed into the branches of the tree fifty metres upstream. He studied their brilliant plumage and stored everything away for future use.

Three hours went by and the shadows began to lengthen. Evening was approaching and soon animals would come to drink. Somewhere out there he knew there was food. The little breeze that was feathering the water in the middle of the river carried with it the musty scent of cattle. He concentrated, straining to detect the familiar sound of hooves.

Later, he heard a faint splash. The sort of splash an animal might make if it had stooped to drink at an unfamiliar place and had misjudged its footing. A splash like that might mean the arrival of new animals. Animals who would not know that this was his territory! Newcomers in a kingdom in which he knew the firmness of every sandbar, the gradient of every river bank and the land beyond for fifty metres.

Steep slopes meant that an animal would waste precious moments leaping upwards to get away from him. Mud or wet sand that would suck at their heels and hold them back for that vital fraction of a second when his attack came in.

Silently, he drifted out into the middle of the river. It was time to investigate further.

Seven

'Always bang your boots on the ground before you put 'em on,' said Sam.

'Why?' asked Tom, watching him.

'So you don't put your stupid toes on something nasty!' Greg snapped. He cracked the heels of his riding boots together then flipped them upside down. Nothing fell out but Greg went on shaking them just to make sure.

Sam grinned at Tom, his teeth gleaming in the light of the pressure lamp. 'Lot of creatures move round in the dark,' he explained. 'Things that like warmth.'

'He means spiders and snakes,' put in Greg, tugging on his boots.

'Snakes like to get in the sleeping bag with you,'

said Sam. 'And spiders head straight for the toes of your boots. Hey! I'm being serious,' he warned, seeing Tom's disbelieving face. 'Ain't that so, Mr Bradley?'

'Sounds about right,' said Bob, putting his head round the tent door. 'Just making sure you fellows are up. We've a lot to do today. So grab some tucker and let's be having you.'

Outside, it was still dark. Tom was surprised how cold it was. His eyes felt tired and gritty. There was also a growing knot of worry in the pit of his stomach. No one had told him what he'd be doing. What if he made a mess of things? He shivered and followed the others down to the cookhouse.

The cookhouse was just two walls and a sagging tin roof. An old army cooker had been dug into the ground and a jet of flame roared away under a row of battered metal containers. Sparks flew high into the branches of an overhanging gum tree.

They joined the queue of hungry stockmen and waited in line for breakfast. A man with a large metal ladle dolloped stew on to his plate. Tom stared at it, looked round at the others then began wolfing it down. They ate standing up using spoons to shovel it in. Afterwards, he copied the others and wiped

35

his plate clean with a hunk of bread. Hot sweet tea came from another dixie.

The stockmen talked together quietly or yawned. Here and there a match flared followed by the smell of cigarette smoke. Bob Bradley finished talking to Jacko. He looked up at the sky. It was suddenly getting light. He put his hands to his mouth and shouted, 'OK! Saddle up! Let's get moving!'

With rising excitement, Tom watched the bustle of activity as the men moved out. Five minutes later, a file of stockmen trotted past. One of them gave Tom a friendly wave. Greg was busy altering the length of his stirrups and ignored him.

There was a cloud of steam as one of the cooks threw the dirty washing-up water over the remains of last night's camp fire. Then, he turned the burner off and there was a sudden deafening silence.

'Ever been in a chopper before?' Bob asked him. And seeing the expression on Tom's face, clapped him on the shoulder and said, 'Always a first time. Just stick close.'

Tom followed his uncle's tall figure for a hundred metres to where the small helicopter was parked. Bob bent and untied the tapes holding the rotor blades down. The blades sprang up, quivering. He walked round the small, white-painted machine carefully checking it over. Then he opened a door and motioned Tom inside.

He started the helicopter with the turn of a key. It was like being in a car. As the roar of the engine built up, the rotor blades began to swing. Slowly at first, then in a blur. The noise was deafening. The helicopter was shaking and bouncing up and down on its skids. Outside, a dust storm raged.

Bob touched his arm and indicated a headset. Tom put it on and heard his uncle talking to him.

'Strapped in?'

He nodded and put up both thumbs in excitement. With a final look around, Bob opened the throttle and the helicopter began to rise. At tree-top height it hesitated, its nose pointing steeply downwards. Tom gripped the sides of his tiny seat and hung against his safety harness. Slowly Bob turned the machine through ninety degrees checking the compass heading as he did so. Then they swooped away, gathering speed all the time.

Eight

The helicopter's shadow raced ahead of them. A flock of birds fanned out from the top branches of a tree. Bob eased the helicopter upwards. 'Got to watch out for that,' he told Tom. 'A bird strike on a machine this size can wreck a blade. And then we'd be in real trouble!'

A new voice cut in over the headset. Tom thought it was Jacko's.

'Great!' his uncle acknowledged. He looked over at Tom. 'Did you get that?' he asked. 'They're ready for us . . . Oh! And if you feel like being sick, there's a bag beside you!'

They dropped into a tight right-hand turn and Tom felt his eyeballs blurring. The safety straps dug in as the ground rushed up towards them. Then they were level again and flashing over scrubby bushes and wide patches of sand.

'The herd should be dead ahead. Couple of miles at the most,' Bob was telling him. 'Give us a shout as soon as you see them.' The radio crackled again. Bob swore. 'The road-trains are arriving. Grief! They're hours too early.'

Tom knew what road-trains were. He had seen them on the way from the airport. They were the trucks that towed two or even three huge trailers two thousand miles or more to the cattle markets in the south. Greg's vehicle had been buffeted from side to side each time one of the great lorries had thundered past, its stainless steel exhausts spewing smoke trails high above the cab.

'There they are!' Bob exclaimed, stabbing a finger.

Tom stared ahead searching for the herd. From the corner of his eye he noticed a small plume of dust and the next moment saw a stockman spurring on his horse.

Then they were looking straight down on what looked like a great river of tossing horns. On either flank, stockmen were riding up and down cracking their long whips, keeping the herd bunched together. The noise of the helicopter hovering in the rear panicked the cattle, and they began to stream after the lead bull. Bob came in even lower. The herd began to break into a shambling run.

'Hang on tight!' Bob warned and laid the machine over on its side. Tom's knuckles gleamed white as he struggled to keep upright. He thought of Greg somewhere down there and wondered if he was enjoying it.

They flew from side to side across the back of the herd. After a couple of minutes, Bob pulled back the stick and they climbed high into the blue sky. 'See the pens?' he shouted, pointing ahead. 'That's where we're driving them.'

Half a mile ahead, Tom could see long panels of sacking nailed to trees and wooden stakes. They formed the mouth of an enormous funnel. The cattle were going to be channelled through it into an huge holding pen a hundred metres beyond. Smaller pens led off on either side. Tom wondered what they were for. Behind some of them, he could see the road-trains waiting and the sun flashing on their windscreens.

Bob was busy again on the radio, directing operations. Then a thought occurred to Tom. Just how were the men going to get all these thousands of cattle into the funnel? What happened if the herd refused and started to scatter? The men couldn't possibly stop them. Already the leading animals were slowing to a walk, looking suspiciously at the panels.

As if reading his thoughts, his uncle pointed to a line of 4×4s hidden behind bushes on either side of the funnel. 'Just watch this!' Bob told him. 'This is where it gets really hairy!' He gave Tom a quick grin and looked down.

'Go! Now!' he suddenly shouted into the radio.

Seconds later, the 4×4s came bouncing out of their cover in clouds of blue exhaust. They drove straight at the herd, braking and slewing sideways at the very last minute, panicking the animals and forcing them into the jaws of the funnel. The helicopter wheeled and circled and the horizon leapt at them from all sides. Ashen-faced Tom hung on.

Bob was talking continuously while they lurched and fell around the sky. Tom suddenly saw a huge bull turn and charge one of the vehicles. For a split second, it lifted the vehicle clear of the ground.

Another 4×4 with a massive bull-bar on its front bumper rammed it. The bull went down poleaxed. The force of the blow rolled it right over. It slithered on its side back into the stream of cattle. For a moment, it looked as if it was going to be trampled by the herd. But they parted just long enough to allow it to stagger to its feet and be carried along with the rest of them.

'Beef like that's worth a lot of money,' Bob observed. Tom said nothing. He felt sorry for the animal.

In a surprisingly short time the herd was penned up. The riders spurred their horses alongside the last few reluctant steers and drove them in. Bob shot a grin at Tom. He was looking pleased. 'Not bad!' he grinned. 'Not bad at all. But this is where the work really starts! So let's go down and give 'em a hand.'

Nine

A thick cloud of dust hung over the stockpens. It towered up into the sky and could be seen for miles. Tom soaked a bandana in water and tied it back over his nose. Dust lay like fur on his tongue. It gummed up his eyes and puffed out his hair. When he crawled into his sleeping bag at night, he could feel it sifting down his shoulders and into the small of his back.

He had never been so tired in all his life. Three days of continuous work and he was dead on his feet. Right now, he would give his right arm for just ten minutes' sleep. Instead, he went on taking round pails of drinking water and mugs of tea and waited until the men had gulped them down.

Sam beckoned to him. He cupped a hand and shouted in Tom's ear, 'You got a nickname!' Tom stared at him uncomprehendingly. Sam chuckled and gave him a thumbs-up. 'The boys are calling you "Mickey".'

Tom shook his head. 'Why?'

'It's what they call the young bulls. Lots of spirit. But that's before they get castrated!' He grinned and winked. Beneath the dust and sweat, Tom flushed with pleasure. His heart swelled and he grinned back at Sam.

He looked round and wished his parents and his school mates could see him now. The air was full of the sound of frightened cattle bellowing and the shouts and curses of the stockmen. Smoke rose from the fires where the branding irons glowed red. The smell of burnt hide and hair was everywhere.

No one back home would ever believe it. He had a camera with him but everyone was far too busy to waste their time taking tourist photographs of himself. Sam might but Tom didn't feel he could ask.

At last, it was all over. The final road-train bumped its way back down to the highway and the remainder of the herd were left to graze for another year. They all shook hands with the men who would be staying out for another couple of days. Bob and

Jacko were going straight back by helicopter.

Sam drove while Greg and Tom promptly fell asleep. After an hour they reached the tarmac road. It was an awkward turn. The road was narrow and on a sharp bend beside a high jumble of rocks.

Sam stopped, glanced casually to his right and pulled out. Some sixth sense made him look again. The next moment he was standing on the brakes with a force that sent Tom pitching on to the floor in the back.

Less than fifty metres away, a van came tearing round the bend on screeching tyres. It was going like a rocket. For a split second Sam thought it was going to tip over. Then, still swaying dangerously, it roared towards them.

Sam's eyes bulged. There was no sign of the driver! Then he saw the back of the man's head. Whatever he was doing, he hadn't seen them! He obviously had no idea they were there at all!

'Back up!' Greg screamed.

'I can't! We've got the trailer on,' Sam yelled back. 'We're stuck!' A few more seconds and the van would smash straight into his door. Sweat ran down his face. There wasn't even time to jump clear. He jammed his hand on the horn.

'Get out! Get out!' Greg was shouting.

The driver's face suddenly appeared, his mouth opening wide in shock. Helpless, Sam watched him wrenching at the steering wheel. In a dream, Sam saw the front wheels starting to turn and the contorted face of the man shouting at them. Greg hid his face in his hands. There was a huge rushing whirlwind of noise. Sam felt the front of their vehicle lift as the van thundered past centimetres away. It seemed to take forever to get past.

Stunned, they sat rooted to their seats watching the van drive on. A bottle sailed out of the driver's window and burst in the road behind. The van did not stop.

Sam let out a low moan of relief and sank his head on the steering wheel. In the back, Tom picked himself up and nursed his elbow. 'Come on! Get after him!' Greg shouted. 'What are you waiting for?'

'No way we'll ever catch him,' Sam said wearily. 'We've not got any speed. The trailer's too heavy.'

'There's a big can of kerosene come loose,' Tom interrupted. 'It's leaking everywhere. All over the sleeping bags and things.'

Sam slewed round. He had forgotten the boy! 'You OK Tom?'

Tom nodded. 'I'm all right. But it's a real mess back here!'

Greg pounded the seat in frustration. 'That guy was drinking! If I ever meet him again, I'm going to plant one right between his eyes!'

Sam looked up and shook his head. 'Forget it,' he said. 'He's gone now. Better get off the road and get things sorted.'

Ten

In the research station, Coyle looked up at the clock on his office wall. He checked his own watch then drummed his fingers impatiently on the desk top. The backs of his hands were covered with tufts of black hair. The phone call came through exactly on the hour. He licked his lips and pressed the security button. Direct contact with these people made even him feel nervous.

'Yes!' he said hoarsely.

A woman's voice answered. He made notes while she gave him his instructions. The rendezvous tomorrow would be with a container ship. Same place, same time, the same procedures as before. The ship would launch a boat and pick up the consignment. He nodded in relief. It would be a straightforward trip. Danny and Merv, the huge guard, could easily handle it.

But the woman's next order brought him to his feet in shock. 'We are closing your operation down. Tomorrow's drop will be your last. You will then have four days to get rid of all records. You must burn everything. Is that understood? Nothing must be left. Nothing!'

'But why? Why?' spluttered Coyle. 'It's been going great. I thought you people were pleased.'

She interrupted. 'We think one of our competitors knows about you. So you must move fast. I'm sure you'll understand why.'

Coyle's eyes widened. This was bad news. Very bad. And dangerous! 'What about the staff?' he demanded.

'Pay them off. The money has already been transferred to your account. But the scientist Dorrell will come back with you. He must not be left behind on any account. He knows too much. But when you are at sea,' she went on, 'you will then get rid of him!'

'But why?' spluttered Coyle. 'He's the brains!'

The woman interrupted angrily. 'Our own chemists now understand his process. He can be

49

disposed of.' Her voice became menacing. 'There must be no mistake about this. If there is we will know who to blame! We will send you further instructions in two days' time.' There was a click and the line went dead.

Coyle stared at the phone. He pushed his chair back and started to pace up and down. Four days wasn't very long. Four days to destroy everything. Then a slow smile began to spread over his face. Only four more days in this dump! He laughed and swung round, lashing out with his foot at a small table. It hit the wall at the end of the room and splintered.

Eleven

After they had re-packed, Greg took over the driving. An hour later, they were climbing a long low hill. As they drove over the crest Greg's loud shout brought the others upright, craning their necks to see what the trouble was.

'Look!' he yelled, pressing the accelerator to the floor. 'Look who it is!'

Halfway down the hill, a grey-painted van had skidded off the road and gone into a drainage ditch. It was tilted to one side. The tyres had gouged deep tracks in the orange-coloured sand.

'It's the same van!' Greg cried in triumph. 'No mistake!'

'There's the driver,' Tom shouted, pointing between their heads.

'Gotcha!' said Greg.

The man was wiry with a thin, pinched face. He wore a grubby singlet and an old pair of shorts. In one hand he held a cigarette and in the other, a CB radio handset.

'He's talking to someone,' said Sam.

As they came level, the man waved them on.

'He doesn't want us to stop,' said Tom.

'Have I got news for him,' Greg muttered, braking to a halt. He was out of the door and striding towards the man in one long, angry movement.

'You stay out of this Tom!' Sam warned, then ran after him.

The driver was about forty with a lot of stubble round his chin. He gave Greg a shifty grin. He had put the microphone back on the seat and was opening a can of beer.

'Thanks for stopping, sport!' he said. 'But I'm OK. Got me mates coming to help. Be here any minute. They're local.' And he raised the can to his lips. His adam's apple bobbed up and down as he drank. He gave a sigh of satisfaction and wiped the back of his hand across his mouth. 'Cripes,' he added. 'I needed that.'

'Like a hole in your stupid head!' Greg stormed.

The man's eyes narrowed. 'Hey sonny! Who the hell d'you think you're talking to?'

Greg's face darkened. He was a good head taller than the driver and obviously much stronger. He moved a step closer and pushed his face into the man's.

'You drunken little creep. You nearly killed us back there. Remember!' He pushed the driver up against the van.

Quick as a flash the man stuck an arm down beside his seat and came up with a wicked-looking knife. It glinted as he turned it over in his hand.

'Back off!' he ordered with venom in his voice. 'Back off!' At that moment, a large American jeep skidded to a halt beside them in a shower of small stones.

Greg shot a surprised glance over his shoulder. The driver lunged. Greg yelled and leapt back. Sam grabbed him and pulled him away.

The jeep's suspension was still swaying as two men got out. They stood together in silence taking in the scene. One was small and had lost the lobe of his right ear. It gave him an odd, lop-sided appearance. The other was a mountain of a man. He had cropped hair and thick sunglasses. He wore a drab shirt and army-style lace-up boots. The smaller man called him Merv.

Tom stared open-mouthed at them. He shivered. Greg had better back down fast, he thought, and be very careful what he said.

'What the hell's going on?' the small man demanded, glaring at the driver.

Before either Sam or Greg could say anything the driver began shouting. 'Don't blame me. It's these jokers. Forced me off the road. Wasn't my fault!' he complained. 'Didn't have a chance.'

'He pulled a knife!' yelled Greg pointing at the driver. 'I'm getting on to the police right now about all this!'

'And he's drunk,' put in Tom.

'Sort it, Merv!' the small man ordered, looking up at him.

Merv walked towards the driver. Greg moved out of his way. Merv held out a hand for the knife and tossed it away into the bush. Then he went back to the jeep and began dragging out the winch cable. 'You!' he shouted at the driver. 'Come here!' The man scuttled over.

The small man with the misshapen ear spread his hands and smiled an apology at Greg. 'The name's

Danny,' he said. 'And I'm so sorry about this. Let me assure you this man will never work for me again. He's just a local contractor. This is all very regrettable. Please, there is no need to bother the police. I'll take care of everything.'

Greg looked over at Sam. Sam's face was expressionless. He said nothing. They watched in silence as Merv paid out the winch. The van driver ducked under the tailboard and shackled it on. 'Keep clear!' Merv ordered and switched the motor on. There was a grating noise and the cable became rigid as it took the strain. The van creaked then came slowly swaying up out of the ditch. For one moment, Tom thought it was going to tip over. But it settled back on the road with a heavy thump.

Greg shrugged. 'Time to be going,' he murmured to Tom. 'No point messing with these people.' He looked round for Sam.

But Sam was standing beside the van staring at it with a puzzled expression on his face. As Greg watched, Sam leaned against the side of the vehicle and cupped his ear, listening intently. He gave a sharp hiss of disbelief. Abruptly, he swung round and faced Danny.

'What you got in here?' he demanded, banging

the flat of his hand against the metal side in a loud tattoo.

'Hey you!' shouted Merv. 'Get out of it!'

Fury spread across Sam's face. 'You've got animals inside!' he screamed. 'Animals in this heat. With no air. Savages!' he swore at them.

Danny scowled. 'Who the hell are you calling a savage?' he shouted back. Then to Greg, 'This guy work for you? Who is he?'

Sam stormed towards him. 'The name's Sam Minamurra, mate. And this is my country you're in! This van's stuffed with animals. In this heat that's criminal! I'm telling the cops!'

'Now wait!' shouted Danny. 'Let's just keep this friendly, shall we?' He looked at them all in turn, trying to force a smile. 'OK. Your man's right. There are some animals in there. But they're only rabbits for heaven's sake. We need them for vital scientific research. They've only got a few miles to go then they'll be well cared for. I promise you.'

But there was no stopping Sam now. He ran back to the van. 'No more waiting. They need help now!' He began wrenching at the long door handles, trying to force them open. Suddenly there was violence everywhere. A lot of it.

Merv pounded towards him. He grabbed Sam by the shirt and the seat of his trousers, plucking him away from the van. Sam writhed and struggled but the big man was far too strong. He held him in a vice-like grip.

'This your fella?' he shouted at Greg. 'Needs to learn a few lessons. Maybe you should have brought him up better!' And he threw Sam bodily into the ditch.

Greg and Tom raced to Sam's help. Greg jumped down into the ditch. Tom followed. They got their arms under Sam's shoulders and pulled him upright. 'Nothing broken,' Sam told them in a shaky voice. He tried to grin. 'Tough old bird, Sam Minamurra.' They helped him out and brushed him down. Tom saw the tears in his eyes and knew they were from pride. He handed him back his old battered trilby.

Sam put it on. 'Let's go home,' he muttered.

They looked round. All the men had gone. 'Did anyone get their registration numbers?' Tom asked.

Greg shook his head. 'Too much dust. Anyway, let's tell the cops what's happened. We've got a good enough description for cripes' sakes! Come on!' But someone had ripped the microphone leads out of their two-way radio.

Twelve

Much later that night, a hot wind came out of the Great Desert. It blew northwards, hugging the land and tumbling over the thornbush like so much thistledown. Snakes buried their heads deep inside their coils and delayed their hunt for food until it had passed.

It flung sheets of grit and sand against the windows of Sam's cabin where he sat cross-legged on the floor. He was honing the blade of his favourite knife. Every now and then he would draw the blade across his thumb to test its sharpness. It had been his father's knife many years ago. There was magic in it and that comforted him.

He crooned to himself the songs of his people. A people that had been old thousands of years before the white man had found these shores and who would still be there, long after he had departed. He listened to the wind and knew it would be gone before dawn.

That was good. Tomorrow, he would go with Greg and young Tom and take them to the land by the sea. Bob had agreed and was happy. They would meet the people of his family. They would hold a corroboree with celebrations and dancing. Sam smiled and his voice grew stronger. He was a fine dancer.

He grinned at the thought of the holiday and kissed the blade of his knife. Reverently, he slid it back in its sheath. Then he lay down and went to sleep.

'Right! Let's have you!' Bob Bradley shouted. Sam waved an arm and Greg drove a heavily-laden 4×4 out of a barn. Jacko put his hands on his hips and whistled. 'Going somewhere?' he called to Tom. 'Bet you've forgotten the can opener!'

Tom grinned. They had spent all of yesterday loading the vehicle. By the time they had finished, it was pitch dark outside. When it was finally over, Sarah had cooked them a huge mixed grill and packed them off to bed. Tom looked at the vehicle now and felt a thrill of satisfaction. They had done a good job.

A steel tow chain and two thick nylon ropes were lashed to the front bumper. The roof rack was piled high with tents, sleeping bags, cooking equipment and boxes of tinned food. Sam had bolted a second spare wheel to the rear door and there were jerricans of petrol stacked in cages on either side.

Inside the truck, there were boxes of spare parts and a brand new battery. There were spanners and cans of oil, shovels and a pickaxe and as many water containers as they had been able to squeeze in under the seats.

'Right! Hold it there,' shouted Bob Bradley, putting up a hand. He gave Tom a wink. 'So let's see what you fellows have forgotten.'

Greg handed him the stores list. His father studied it carefully. 'Let's have a look at your medical kit,' he demanded. 'Not enough water purifying tablets for a start,' he told them, a couple of minutes later. 'You'll need twice as many. And you should still boil your water whenever you can,' he added, 'just in case some bush rat's been there before you.'

'Now let's see if you've taken a set of distributor

points with you,' he said. 'And while you're at it, show me your spare fanbelt.'

Greg found the fanbelt almost at once. The points took a lot longer. He was getting hot and bothered before he remembered stowing them away in a small cardboard box beside the heavy-duty jack.

Bob pushed his hat to the back of his head and scratched his brow. 'If I was you,' he said pleasantly, 'I'd keep everything electrical together. Same applies to your oils and your fuel. Just makes things easier to find.' While Greg repacked, Sam opened the bonnet and Bob checked the radiator hoses.

Sarah drew Tom to one side. 'Greg tells me you've been doing your homework on survival techniques.'

Tom nodded. She smiled at him. 'So just put my mind at rest, will you?'

'I'll try,' he replied. A kookaburra landed on a wooden post twenty metres away. A long peal of demented laughter filled the yard. It was an eerie sound. One of the stockmen threw his hat at it and it flew off still screaming.

'Ask Sam about those birds,' Sarah told him. 'He's got some weird stories. Now young man! What's the golden rule if your vehicle breaks down in the bush?'

Tom grinned. He knew this one. The others had

drummed it into him. 'You MUST stay with it,' he replied.

'But what if there's a range of hills in sight. With trees and shade. Maybe a stream?' she persisted. 'And you reckon you could walk it easy in a couple of hours?'

'No!' Tom shook his head. 'You've got to stay with the vehicle all the time.'

'Why?' she asked. 'Sounds crazy to me.'

'Because it's much easier for rescuers to see a vehicle from the air than find a person down on the ground on their own.'

'Good,' she said. 'Oh! And don't forget there's some emergency flares in a box by the back door. OK. Now try this one. You're out there on your own. Your water's almost gone and you'll be dead of thirst in another day. Tell me one thing you can do to get water.'

'Get a plastic bag from the vehicle. Find a gum tree and slip it over the thickest bunch of leaves you can reach. Tie it on very tightly. And you'll get a litre of fluid every four hours while the sun's up.'

'Good.' She sounded pleased. 'Last question. The Flying Doctor. When do you call him out?'

'Only when it's a matter of life or death,' Tom told

her. 'Broken arms don't count. That's what you told me!'

'I should think not,' she agreed. 'Now come and show me how to work the radio.' On their way over to the vehicle she said, 'Do you know the frequency for the doctor around here?'

'Yes. I was listening in to you the other day.' She watched while he switched the receiver on and tuned the set. 'That's the midwife talking,' she told him a few moments later. Then smiled at him. 'You learn quick. That's good. Now, where's your uncle got to?'

She and Bob talked together for a few moments. Greg, Sam and Tom watched them with rising excitement.

'Dad!' called Greg, unable to control his impatience any longer.

His father came over and looked at them all in turn. 'As long as you promise faithfully to radio in every night at six . . . well . . . I guess you chaps can go. So have a good time . . .' But the rest of what he said was drowned in all the noise.

Thirteen

The research station was at the end of a long track. It lay in a hollow surrounded by gum trees. From the tarmac road, there was very little to see. A small sign had been put out but it was easy to miss.

The barrier at the main entrance was flung upwards. It hit a restraining bar and came crashing down again. The black jeep braked hard and Danny bit his tongue. The guard grinned sheepishly and lifted the pole up again. As they drove through he sketched a salute.

'Has that guy got any brains at all?' Danny demanded, dabbing at his mouth with a silk handkerchief.

The big man, Merv, laughed. 'Well, he's not exactly Einstein . . . but he's handy in a fight!'

Danny muttered something inaudible and Merv leant towards him. 'Hey! Relax. He's just the sort of bloke you need for this job. That's why you hired him. Me too, for pete's sake! Mind if I smoke?'

Without waiting for an answer, he produced a new packet and ripped away the cellophane with his teeth. He tried to spit it out of the window but it kept blowing back in his face. Danny had been meaning to tell him for the last two months to close the window first.

On the seat between them lay a sealed waterproof container the size of a microwave oven. It was bright orange in colour and weighed five kilograms. This, Merv reflected, was what it was all about. The operation had gone well. Just this final drop to make and then they'd be away out of it.

Coyle had told him last night that the place was closing down. Danny thought it made good sense. If some other syndicate really had discovered what they were doing out here, then the sooner they got out the better. Danny wondered if Dorrell had told someone. The man was unreliable. He had always said so. He drank too much for a start.

'Feel like a cheese sandwich?' Merv asked. 'They're

fresh.' Danny shook his head and they drove the next five miles in silence.

'River coming up,' Merv warned. 'Hang on.' He swung off the road and began bumping towards a line of bushes some three hundred metres ahead. Danny looked back to check the boat was steady on its trailer.

The boat was a four-metre-long dinghy with a shiny aluminium hull. It was powered by a huge Johnson outboard engine. It could do almost twenty miles an hour in a calm sea but along the river they kept the speed down. There were too many sand bars.

A pair of crows heard the jeep coming. They hopped clumsily into the air and flew up to the top of a tree. They sat with heads to one side watching the approaching plume of dust. Men usually left things to scavenge.

Danny and Merv eased the dinghy off its trailer and carried it down to the water's edge. Next, they lifted the heavy outboard up on to the boat's transom. Merv kept it steady while Danny secured it in place with two thick steel pins.

Merv stared at the river. 'Keep your eyes skinned for crocs,' he said casually. Danny shivered involuntarily.

'Go get the box,' he ordered and watched Merv scramble back up the bank. Danny waded waist deep round to the bow, checking for leaks or any sign of damage. Behind him, the river moved silently towards the sea. Merv reappeared with the container cradled in his arms. He placed it carefully in the middle of the boat. 'I'll park the jeep,' he told Danny and walked away, whistling.

It suddenly went very still. No human being could have detected the change but the crows sensed it at once. They tightened their hold on the branch as if a cold wind was ruffling their feathers. They stared down at the river.

Danny felt something brush his leg. He gave a start and stooped down, peering into the water. Weed! Of course! There was a lot of it around here. Sometimes it fouled the propeller. He relaxed and put his head back. He closed his eyes and enjoyed the feel of the sun on his face. Soon he could take a holiday. A whole month perhaps? In Rio, why not? That would be wonderful. He smiled at the thought.

There was a loud splash. The hair on his neck lifted. He flung himself round, slipping on a stone as he did so and almost falling. He grabbed at the bow and hung on. Large ripples were racing towards him. Danny froze, his eyes wide with fear, scanning the surface.

There was a guffaw of laughter further along the bank. 'Only a rock, mate! Just keeping the crocs away. Didn't mean to give you a fright!'

Merv held the dinghy steady while Danny clambered in. Danny banged his shin on a thwart and swore explosively. The engine caught at the second attempt with a roar and a puff of blue smoke. Furious, Danny opened the throttle and they surged away, the wash slapping at the bank.

Behind them in the middle of the river, there was a slow swirl in the water. For a fleeting second, a terrible head reared up, staring after them. Then the long jaws closed and Kyrek sank back under the boat's wake and disappeared from sight.

Fourteen

On the second floor of police headquarters in Darwin, Sergeant MacIntyre stared out of his window. He sipped a mug of tea and frowned. He had known Bob Bradley and his family for years. He had no reason at all to doubt Greg's story and in any case both the Aborigine and the British kid had backed him up.

He went over to his computer and ran through the police wanted list again. There was no one recorded there with an ear lobe missing. The more he thought about it the more uneasy he became. Those men in the jeep and that van driver with the knife. The boys had been lucky. So had Sam Minamurra come to that.

But just why had the big man become so

aggressive? What could be that important about a vanload of rabbits? Perhaps old Sam had got that bit wrong. He must have done. It didn't make any sense as it was. All the same, thought Sergeant MacIntyre, he'd have a word with one or two people because he knew in his bones there was something nasty going on. And he wanted to know more about it. Much more.

Fifteen

'This is fantastic!' Tom cried, gripping the steering wheel tight in excitement. 'I thought sand would be all loose to drive on. This is just like being on a road!'

'You wait,' said Sam.

They were speeding along following an old set of wheel tracks. The noise of the tyres filled the cab. Ahead of them, a ridge of sand dunes towered up against a brilliant blue sky.

'Watch out!' Greg shouted.

Too late, Tom saw the pothole ahead. The wheel whipped away from under his fingers. He wrestled to bring it back under control. For a moment nothing happened and they slewed to one side. Then the tyres gripped and the 4×4 straightened up. A puff of dust marked the spot.

Greg pulled out a fresh packet of chewing gum. 'Just keep following the tracks,' he drawled. 'And not so fast or you'll have us over.'

Chastened, Tom settled back into the driver's seat and concentrated as hard as he could. They drove in silence for a while. His thumb was bruised from the whiplash of the steering wheel.

'Maybe three hours to the river crossing,' Sam told Greg.

'Don't speak too soon,' Greg warned. 'We've still got the dunes to get over.'

Outside, the sun glared down and the heat rolled over them in waves. It was like being in a furnace. There was no sign of life. There were no birds, no animals. The only vegetation was the odd parched-looking thorn bush. The 4×4 was a tiny black dot utterly alone in an ocean of sand and rock.

The dunes were closing in around them. The going was getting steeper all the time. Tom changed down a gear and followed the tracks round in a long, climbing turn. The vehicle pitched from side to side tossing the three of them together.

'You're doing fine!' Sam called and put his arm round Tom's shoulders.

But Tom hardly heard him. Instead, he was staring in horror at a huge sandhill towering ahead of them. He let out a gasp and looked wildly for a way around. Sam slapped his hand on the dashboard and chuckled.

'It's the big fella,' he called. 'Hey! Looks like he's put on some weight!'

'We can't drive over that!' Tom cried in alarm.

'Don't slow down!' Greg warned. 'You'll get stuck. Keep going!'

The dune loomed over them, its surface scalloped into countless waves by the wind.

'Where? Which way!' Tom shouted in sudden anger.

'There is no way round!' Greg told him. 'You've just got to keep going straight on up. It's no sweat. We've done it tons of times, haven't we Sam?'

Sam nodded. 'He's not as bad as he looks. We'll put you right. Don't worry.'

'Keep her in second gear and get your revs up,' Greg advised.

Tom hardly heard him. His heart was racing and his mouth had gone bone dry. The dune rose to meet them. Its crest far out of sight. The tyres drummed loudly gripping the surface and thrusting them upwards. Sweat poured down Tom's face. It stung his eyes but he dared not take a hand off the wheel to wipe it away. He hated heights. He had never been so frightened in all his life.

Blindly he drove on. It grew steeper and steeper until there was only blue sky to be seen at the end of the bonnet. Which meant they must almost be at the top! With all that way down beneath them! A terrifying picture flashed through his mind. He had only to make one mistake and they would roll backwards . . . faster and faster . . .

'Watch your revs,' warned Greg pointing at the instrument panel.

Tom jammed his foot on the accelerator. 'Not that much!' Greg shouted.

The engine began to labour. 'Change down!' someone was yelling. Tom missed the gear. The nightmare was coming true. The vehicle lurched. The back end slewed round spitting out sheets of sand as the rear wheels broke through the surface crust. The engine stalled and they came to an abrupt halt.

'I'm sorry! I'm so sorry,' Tom gasped, his eyes hot with mortification.

'Damn right!' Greg swore. 'Now you can dig us out of this mess!'

Sixteen

Danny throttled back the engine and turned towards a battered-looking fishing boat anchored in the middle of Woomerloo Sound. Behind them, a dark line of mangroves stretched away on either side of the river mouth. Out here, little waves sparkled in the sunshine and the smell of the sea filled their nostrils.

'Get ready to hook on,' he called a few minutes later. Merv raised a large hand in acknowledgement. Danny cut the engine and brought the dinghy in close to the fishing boat. The name on her stern said *Bluewater*.

Danny measured the distance then briefly put the engine into reverse. The dinghy came to a stop and lay rocking gently alongside the fishing boat.

Merv stood up, steadied himself against the hull then clambered up on to *Bluewater*'s deck. Danny flung him a mooring line and he made the dinghy fast.

Carefully, Danny handed up the bright orange container. Then he too pulled himself up and joined Merv.

'Feeling better?' Merv chided. Then he laughed and slapped Danny on the arm. 'Come on,' he said. 'It was only a joke. Tossing a rock into the river's an old trick. I can't believe you'd fall for it.'

Danny made a face. 'That's better,' Merv encouraged. 'Hey, relax! There's nothing to worry about. This trip's going to be easy.'

Danny gave a weak grin. The big man was right. It just showed how tense he must be. 'OK,' he said. 'No offence taken.' He looked at his watch. 'Let's get the engines started.'

Twenty minutes later, the *Bluewater* was rising and falling in the ocean swell. Her engines were purring sweetly and her wake stretched out behind them. Danny checked the chart and made a quick calculation.

He put his head out of the wheelhouse. 'Three hours to go.'

Merv sat in the sun outside, a can of beer in his hand. 'So who we expecting at the pick-up this time?' he asked.

'Container ship,' Danny told him. 'Big job with a green hull. We've used her before. You'll recognize her.' He checked the compass heading again. The tide was turning and starting to push them back in towards the land. Gently he turned the spokes of the wheel to counter it. Just this one last rendevous to make and then he could really relax. He would have done his job. No one could blame him now. He opened the throttle still further and felt the deck vibrating beneath his feet.

Merv looked in, blocking the doorway. He raised his beer can with a flourish. 'This is the life,' he called. 'I'm really going to miss you people when you've gone. Cheers!'

Seventeen

'Right!' said Sam squatting down beside a back wheel. 'The first thing to do is to let the tyres down.'

'Why?' asked Tom.

'The more tyre you have on the ground,' said Greg, wiping his nose on the back of his hand, 'the more you spread the vehicle's weight over the sand.'

'So the wheels won't dig in as much,' added Sam.

'Why didn't we do that before?' Tom questioned.

Sam looked up at Greg. Then he laughed. 'He's right!' he said.

'I need a drink,' Greg scowled. 'There's still some in the ice box. Let's all have one.' The three of them stood on top of the dune drinking cold shandy in silence while the air shimmered around them. Greg avoided Tom's eye.

'Nobody worry,' said Sam, crinkling up his empty can. 'Happens all the time.' He clapped Greg on the shoulder. 'For you too, my friend.'

Greg nodded. 'Yeah ... well ... I suppose,' he said grudgingly.

'Come on then! Let's start!' Sam cried encouragingly and handed Tom a shovel. It was back-breaking work and took far longer than Tom had expected. The sand below the crust was very fine and kept collapsing inwards. By the time they cleared the back wheels, Tom had a large blister coming up on the palm of his hand.

'OK. Let's take a breather,' Sam suggested. They had another drink while the sweat ran down their chests. Greg rummaged in the front of the vehicle and came out holding a baseball cap. 'Stick this on,' he said thrusting it at Tom. 'No point getting sunstroke out here.'

When they had got their breath back, Sam told them to start digging the sand away from the front of the wheels. While they did so, he climbed on to the roof and rummaged through a tool box. He threw down an armful of sacking and some short wooden planks beside each of the wheels and jumped down.

He then got into the driver's seat and started the engine. Greg gave him a thumbs-up. To Tom's surprise, the vehicle began to inch its way backwards down the face of the dune. 'That'll do you!' Greg shouted.

'Come here!' he called to Tom. 'And I'll show you what to do.' Greg lay on his stomach full length on the sand. 'It's dead easy,' he began. 'Lay the sacking in the wheel tracks right up against the front of the tyres. When you've done that lay the planks on top. You do this side, I'll take the other.'

When he was satisfied, Greg gave Sam the thumbs-up. Sam nodded and waved them clear. Then he drove the truck backwards and forwards a few centimetres at a time until the sacking and the planks were well bedded down.

Sam got out and the two of them studied the ground. 'Let's give it a go!' Greg said. 'Feeling strong?' he asked Tom. The engine note increased to a low roar. Slowly, very slowly, Sam let out the clutch. 'PUSH!' screamed Greg, wedging his shoulder up against the tailboard. 'Come on. Heave!'

Tom closed his eyes, took a deep breath and pushed with all his strength. The vehicle began to shake and rock from side to side. Showers of sand shot out from under the sacking whipping at his bare legs. He couldn't tell if the 4×4 was moving or rolling back on top of them. It seemed to hang motionless. Its grinding weight only prevented from toppling downwards by the strength of their bodies.

There was a crash of gears. The vehicle jerked forward, engine howling and Tom pitched forward face down on to the sand. He lay in the wheel ruts too tired to move or even care. Above him, Greg windmilled his arms trying to keep his balance then he too collapsed.

'Well done, mate,' he gasped, sprawling beside Tom. 'We did it.'

Tom felt a rush of pride. It was the first nice thing Greg had said to him. He grinned to himself but didn't reply. He was too exhausted. They lay there a while longer while the pounding in their chests subsided.

'Come on then,' Greg grunted. 'Or Sam'll think we want to stay here.'

Sam had stopped a hundred metres away. He gave them a cheerful grin as they joined him. 'Look over there!' he exclaimed, pointing into the distance. Tom shaded his eyes. Below him the dune fell steeply. Tom felt his stomach churn. Quickly, he followed the direction of Sam's outstretched arm.

'Yep! That's the river all right,' said Greg with satisfaction. He turned to Tom. 'See that black line of trees on the horizon? There's a crossing there we can take.'

Tom nodded then turned to Sam. 'How far from there to your family, Sam?'

'A day if it all goes well,' Sam replied.

'Sam's people live along the shores of Woomerloo Sound,' Greg explained. 'It's where the river joins the sea. It's only a couple of hours as the crow flies from the crossing. Only trouble is we aren't crows and there's a whole lot of mangrove swamp in the way.'

'So we got to drive the long way round,' added Sam.

'Time to be moving then,' said Greg good-naturedly. 'And this time, I'm doing the driving!'

Eighteen

They camped much later that afternoon on top of a low cliff above the river. The river was lined with baobab trees. They reminded Tom of children's drawings with their square-shaped trunks and stubby little branches.

The river glided quietly over polished white boulders. There were lily pads a metre wide with huge purple flowers at their centre. The nearest pads were about thirty metres away. Bright green ferns grew amongst the cracks in the rocky sides.

Tom looked round to see what the others were doing then scrambled down to the river's edge. There was a wide sandy beach on the opposite bank. Tom studied it. It wouldn't take any time to swim there and back and he wanted a swim very badly. He

84

was sweat-stained and tired. There was sand in his hair, under his fingernails and inside his shorts.

He slipped off his shoes and stood ankle deep in the water. He closed his eyes and let the sensation engulf him. The water felt like cool silk. He took a deep breath and slowly let it out. The stress of the day began to disappear. He could stay here for ever, he decided. A bird shrilled from a nearby bush. He waded further out.

'Hey!' Sam's furious shout interrupted his sense of well-being. 'Tom! Get back! What the heck you doing!' He came scrambling down the rocks in a flurry of arms and legs. He grabbed Tom's arm and unceremoniously dragged him away.

'You want to see your mother again?' he hissed, putting his face into Tom's. 'You want to get me into big trouble with Bob and Greg?' He scowled at the boy. 'You think you know better than Sam?'

'Hey look! I'm sorry . . .' began Tom.

'Me too,' Sam snapped. Then he shook his head. 'It's my fault. I forgot to tell you about crocodiles. Saltwater crocodiles. The scariest in the world. I'm a stupid man.'

It was Tom's turn to reassure. 'Don't worry,' he said. 'I had a really good look before I came down.

There was nothing there. I promise you.'

Sam cleared his throat and spat on to the sand. 'See those lily pads?' he pointed, grabbing Tom's arm. 'The crocs hide under there and watch. They don't miss a trick. They can stay there all day, waiting. Then an animal like you comes along and thinks everything is safe.' He clapped his hands together. 'Big mistake!'

He shook his finger at Tom. 'Want to know how bad it is?' he said. 'Most aboriginal families round here have someone taken by a croc every year. It's usually a woman or her child.'

Tom's mouth dropped.

Sam shrugged. 'That's how it goes,' he said with resignation. 'Think you can run fast?' he asked and without waiting for Tom's reply added, 'No man alive can outrun a crocodile. They can do twenty miles an hour over fifty metres.' He grinned suddenly at Tom. 'You get chased by a six-metre-long saltwater with its jaws open, it's time to say goodbye, my friend. Ain't nothing that can help you then.'

'Hey! You guys!' came Greg's voice from above. 'On strike or something? Come and give us a hand! I'm not making camp on my own!'

Sam raised his arm in acknowledgement. He

pushed Tom ahead of him. 'Just stay close to old Sam,' he said, the humour returning to his voice. 'He'll put you right.'

They hurried back to the vehicle. Greg had already unpacked a small mound of stores. They all set to and very quickly had put up the tent, two camp beds and got the food organized.

'Doesn't Sam have a bed?' Tom asked, looking round inside the tent.

Sam shook his head. 'Always sleep on the ground.'

'Keeps the snakes from coming inside!' Greg laughed.

Later, Tom went off with Sam to collect wood for the camp fire. There was plenty lying around and all of it tinder dry. Tom worked steadily picking up branches and dragging them into a pile. He stopped under a tree and took a breather. He looked up and was puzzled to see a number of triangular-shaped leaves hanging down from a branch.

They looked like large samosas. The sort his father liked whenever they went out for a family meal. Tom stared up at them, puzzled. He had never seen leaves this shape or size before. Then he noticed that they weren't just a single leaf but several, all joined together. Intrigued, he picked up a long thin stick and rapped the nearest one.

Seconds later the whole branch was boiling over with enraged ants. But ants of a kind he had never seen before. Bright green ants in their thousands swarmed over every inch of the bark. Some fell on to his arm and he yelled in surprise. It felt as if a dozen red-hot injection needles had suddenly been thrust through his skin. He ran, slapping at them. Sam thought it a great joke and picked a whole lot more from Tom's hair.

'They're bad, those things,' Greg remarked laconically, when they got back to camp. 'Probably sting you to death if enough got hold of you. Bit stupid of you annoying 'em. This isn't Hyde Park, you know.'

Tom said nothing. Greg as usual was right. Then, while Sam went off to check the vehicle, he helped Greg build the fire. Tom watched Greg dig a shallow hole. 'Aren't we going to have a bonfire?' Tom asked.

Greg stared at him. 'Take a look around,' he advised. 'If this place catches fire we're all dead men. Ever seen a bush fire before?'

Tom thought of the muddy paths that criss-crossed the woods back home. He shook his head. How could he?

'You get a wall of fire metres high in a couple of minutes,' Greg told him. 'Goes across the ground faster than you can drive. This way, we keep the sparks to a minimum. In the morning, you just fill it back in with earth. Simple and safe.'

Greg opened a packet of firelighters and pulled one out. Tom saw they were the same brand that his grandmother used at home. He was amused. 'Why aren't you rubbing sticks together or something?' he joked.

Greg looked up at him, puzzled. 'Don't be daft,' he said. 'What do you think matches are for?' Tom smiled to himself but said nothing. Sam appeared carrying a battered saucepan.

'There's corned beef too if you fancy some,' he told them.

'I'll cook if you like,' Tom offered and was pleased when no one objected. Soon he had a large frying pan full of sausages spitting nicely. He opened a couple of cans of baked beans and scraped them into the dented saucepan. Then he cut up some hunks of bread from a large loaf Sarah had put in and buttered them.

'You like cooking, don't you,' Greg stated, watching him.

'Yes,' Tom agreed. 'I do it at school.'

Greg was surprised. 'Funny sort of thing to study I'd have thought.'

'Makes a lot of sense,' said Sam, licking his fingers.

'I'm thinking of becoming a chef,' Tom confided shyly.

'Good job,' put in Sam. 'Never go short of tucker and that's a fact.'

Greg made a face. 'Wouldn't fancy it myself. Indoors too much.'

'So what are you going to do when you're older then?' Tom asked him.

'Take over from the old man, I expect.'

'That'll be the day I go on serious walkabout,' said Sam rolling his eyes in mock horror.

A thought struck Tom. 'Do you go to school in Darwin?'

Greg laughed. 'Wish I did. Get a bit of life. See the girlfriend more.' He shook his head. 'No. I'm just another student of the School of the Air.'

'School of the what?' Tom asked.

'You never heard of it?' Greg looked surprised. 'Kids up country get lessons each day during term time on the radio,' he explained. 'We send in homework and they mark it and send it back out. It's great. You can sit out on the porch and have a coke at the same time.'

Tom considered this and thought of the ugly concrete buildings his own school occupied. Then the sausages began to smoke. 'Scoff's up!' he called. 'Come and get it.' And to his delight they came and had second helpings, too.

Nineteen

Later that evening, long after Greg had radioed Balgarri, they sat gazing into the fire alone with their thoughts. Around them, the gum trees stood like so many motionless grey sentinels while the firelight chased shadows up and down their trunks. They watched and listened to the sounds the fire made, the crackles, the hiss and the soft sigh of ash falling. Despite the immensity of the Southern sky and stars more brilliant than Tom thought possible, the whole world had shrunk into this tiny clearing. It could have been the first day of Creation and themselves, the first people.

'Wonderful thing, fire,' said Tom dreamily, prodding a glowing ember.

'Not when you've seen as many bush fires as

we have, eh Sam?' Greg grunted.

'What I mean is,' Tom went on, 'just imagine how those first people must have felt when they discovered fire. It must have been incredible.'

'Must have been pretty scared of losing it too,' Greg remarked.

'My people believe fire came from the sky,' Sam said quietly. 'Before the Dreamtime.'

'What's the Dreamtime?' Tom asked.

Sam smiled to himself and stared deeper into the fire. A branch shifted and collapsed. A spark leapt upwards and disappeared into the darkness. The scent of the wood was very strong, like incense.

'We believe that at the beginning of this world,' Sam began, 'before there was any life, before anything was here, the land was all flat. No hills, no rivers, no sea. Nothing. There were no people.' He looked over at Tom. 'Then, great giants rose from out of the ground where they had been asleep. These giants walked across the land and they made fire, and they made their camps. They dug for water and they fought each other and they hunted animals.'

He paused and began to rock backwards and forwards, the firelight glowing on his face. There was a long silence before he went on in a low voice they had to strain to hear.

'These people made the hills and the sand. They made rivers and the sea. They gave us the animals to eat and the weapons to catch them. They gave the stones to help grind food. They gave the laws we live by. And then they all left. No one knows why. And the Dreamtime came to an end.' He gave a deep sigh and closed his eyes. There was a pause.

'I like the story of the sunrise,' Greg prompted. 'Tell him that one too.'

Sam changed his position and squatted down on his haunches. He picked up a stick and prodded the fire. He looked enquiringly at Tom who nodded back. 'Please,' he said.

'The first sunrise . . .' Sam considered. 'Well, in the early days,' he began, 'the sky was so close to the ground that it was always dark. Life for every animal was hard. They all had to go on their bellies like snakes, trying to find something to eat but not able to see what it was.

'So the magpies, who are the cleverest birds, met and talked for a long time and decided if they worked together, they could lift up the sky and make more room. Then, all the animals could see and stand up. So they got long sticks and lifted the sky up. They placed rocks under the sticks to keep it there.

'Then they tried to rest the sky on the tops of the hills. And the sky broke wide open and the sun came up and shone through the hole. And the magpies were the first animals to see the sunrise. The darkness broke into little pieces that are now the clouds. The magpies were very pleased with what they had done. And since that day they are still the first birds to see the sunrise and sing thanks to it.'

Tom nodded to himself and hugged his knees in pure contentment.

'Kind of gets you, doesn't it,' said Greg yawning. 'You should tell stories on the television, Sam. Make more money at it than my old man pays you.'

Sam laughed and looked at Tom. 'You liked that?' he asked.

'Yes!' said Tom. 'Tell me more.'

'Tomorrow night,' said Sam.

'Time for bed, I reckon,' said Greg. 'Got another long day before we get to Woomerloo.'

Twenty

Sam was the first to wake the next morning. He lay with his eyes still closed, listening to the sounds of the early day. The earth smelt fresh and cool. There was still a hint of woodsmoke in the air.

He opened his eyes and knew at once that the sun had already cleared the horizon. In another twenty minutes all this freshness would have gone. Burnt off by the remorseless power of the sun. It was time to be moving.

He sat up carefully, moving with deliberate slowness. But there were no snakes curled up beside him. He looked over towards the tent entrance searching the dusty ground for any tell-tale slither marks. But there were none. There was no need to wake the boys up yet.

Silently he left the tent and walked down to the river. It was the picture of tranquillity. He stared down at the place where he and Tom had stood the evening before and studied their footprints. They were undisturbed. There were no other tracks to be seen.

Sam grunted. He walked fifty metres further on, studying the river the whole time. Then he jumped down and splashed water over his face. Next he dipped the kettle he was carrying under the surface. And all the time his eyes never left the river. Back at camp, the fire was not quite out. Sam blew on an ember and soon had a flame licking up the side of the kettle.

Half an hour later, the three of them stood round the fire drinking strong, sweet tea and eating strips of bacon with their fingers. It was delicious.

'Right then!' said Greg licking his thumb. 'Time to break camp. We've got a long way to go, so I suggest we start now.' When they had finished taking down the tent and stowing everything back on the vehicle, Sam threw water on the fire and Tom covered it with sand. Then they checked to make sure the place was clear of rubbish. Greg spread the map over the 4×4's bonnet and they gathered round to look.

'We're heading for the old mission place,' Greg told them. 'That's where Sam's family live. Right Sam?'

Sam nodded and beckoned Tom to come closer. 'Take a look,' he said. Tom watched his finger follow the river into Woomerloo Sound then head due north tracing the shoreline.

'We'll follow the road as far as we can,' Greg told Tom. 'Then we take this track for the remainder. It'll be pretty bumpy along there so let's make sure everything's packed tight. Feel like having first crack at the driving, Sam?'

Half an hour later, they were bowling along a tarmac road. Tom was studying the map. 'Is this the same road we were on after the cattle muster?' he asked.

Greg nodded. 'Sure is,' he agreed. 'Only proper road in a hundred miles. The place that van got stuck is a couple of miles back the other way.'

Sam interrupted them with a loud groan.

'What's the matter?' Greg demanded.

'I smell steam,' Sam told him in a voice full of foreboding.

'Jeez! You're right. Look at the gauge!' Greg exclaimed.

There was no doubt about it. The needle was flickering and climbing towards the red danger level. Sam slowed down and as he did so, clouds of steam began to escape from under the bonnet.

'The radiator's got a hole in it or something,' Sam cried. 'Must be. I filled her right up before we left.'

'Great!' said Greg. 'That's all we need.'

'Look! There's a sign. On the roadside. Dead ahead,' said Tom.

'Where?' Greg demanded. 'I can't see any.'

'Skinwatch Research,' Tom read aloud as they drew nearer.

'Don't make it easy for people to see do they,' Greg grumbled. An arrow had been chalked underneath.

'Must be up that track.' He turned to Sam. 'OK Sam? Let's turn right here. We can fix it when we get there.'

'Fine by me,' said Sam. They drove up the track at a walking pace, blowing steam like an old-fashioned railway engine. Sam kept making faces as each new cloud appeared. They stopped just short of a pole barrier beside a small, brick building. In the compound below, there were a number of long, single-storeyed buildings. None of them had any windows. 'Looks like a chicken farm,' said Greg pushing open his door.

A man came bustling out. He held his hand up to stop them. He was a thickset individual with cropped hair. He wore polished army boots and a brown uniform shirt. Sam stared at him and a shiver of fear ran down his spine. He licked his lips.

'G'day!' Greg called cheerily. 'We've blown our radiator. You got some ramps we could use to take a look underneath?'

The man hooked his thumbs in his belt and shook his head. 'This is private property, mate. You can't come in here. No one can!'

Greg's jaw dropped in disbelief. 'Look,' he said in amazement. 'We're sorry to bother you only we can't go any further until we fix it.'

The guard shrugged. 'That's your problem.'

'I just don't believe this!' Greg exclaimed, banging his fist on the bonnet. 'Listen mate! We're not in the middle of Sydney or London or some other big place. We're miles from anywhere.'

The guard shook his head stubbornly. 'It's more than my job's worth to let you in.'

Greg took a deep breath. 'Well, is there anyone else here who can give us permission? Look . . . we won't be more than half an hour. I promise!'

The man hesitated. 'Well,' he said, scratching his neck, 'the others are all out right now. There's only Dorrell and he's busy in the lab.'

'Couldn't you just tell him we only need a little bit of help. Then we can be on our way and stop being a nuisance to you.'

The man brightened and nodded. 'All right,' he said. 'I'll give him a call and see what he says. But you stay right where you are. Don't come any nearer. I'll be watching. Understand?'

'What sort of place is this!' Tom exclaimed as the guard disappeared inside.

'You know who that man reminds me of?' Greg asked in a low voice.

Sam looked at them both. 'Sure do!' he said quietly. 'That big thug we met last week out by the van.'

'I wonder when he's due back?' Tom exclaimed and then wished he hadn't. An uncomfortable silence fell.

'If they still say no,' Sam told Greg, 'just ask them for a couple of eggs.'

'Eggs?' asked Tom, thinking he couldn't have heard right. 'What you want eggs for?'

Sam tried to smile. Tom stared at him and suddenly noticed how frightened he looked. There was fear in his eyes. There were tiny beads of sweat on his forehead.

'You'll see,' he told Tom. Then he got out of the vehicle and opened the bonnet. 'Keep away!' he ordered as steam billowed out.

'Here's someone now,' Greg called. 'Come and have a look.'

A man in a long white coat was walking up the slope towards them. They watched him approach in silence. A telephone began ringing in the brick gatehouse. 'You just stay put,' the guard warned and went inside to answer it.

The man stopped beside the barrier and looked at them all in turn. Greg thought he was in his late twenties. The guard had called him Dorrell. 'So what's the problem?' he asked.

He was reserved but not unfriendly. He listened in silence then shook his head. 'The guard's right I'm afraid. You can't come in. We're doing top-level research.' He rubbed his chin. 'I'm really sorry about this.'

'Can you spare a couple of eggs then, mate?' Sam demanded gruffly. 'It'll help get us out of here.'

Dorrell stared at him. 'You pulling my leg or something?' he demanded.

Sam shook his head. Dorrell shrugged. 'All right,' he said. 'Wait here. I'll try the cookhouse.' He returned with three eggs. 'In case one's gone bad,' he said with a smile. The guard came out to watch.

Sam pulled a jerrican of water from inside the vehicle and brought it round to the front. Carefully he opened the radiator cap. A plume of steam shot two metres into the air. When it subsided, he poured a little water into the radiator. Next, he cracked all the eggs and slipped them inside. Sam looked round at their mystified faces and winked. He added the rest of the water and asked Greg to start the engine.

'Old bush trick,' he told them. 'The egg white finds the hole and makes a seal. The rest gets cooked. It'll hold a while longer until I fix it proper.'

Dorrell threw back his head and roared with laughter. 'Great stuff!' he called. He put out his hand to shake Sam's then stood stock still. He turned abruptly, ducked under the barrier and hurried back into the compound.

'What the heck—' began Greg. But Sam was

pushing past him and running towards the driver's door. 'Get in! All of you. Get in!' he was shouting.

And then Tom saw why and his heart gave a lurch. A black jeep was turning in off the road. He had no problem remembering when he had last seen it. It was accelerating towards them leaving a plume of dust behind.

Sam turned their vehicle round and waited. He had the engine running and his hand on the gear stick. It was shaking. Helplessly, Tom stared at the approaching jeep and knew it was the only other vehicle in all this wilderness. It braked to a halt in front of them.

Merv got out. He was wearing sunglasses. The small man with the funny ear stayed in the cab. Tom took a deep breath.

'Wait 'til I tell you Sam,' said Greg out of the corner of his mouth.

Merv stood in the middle of the track his hands on his hips. He looked at their number plate, then came towards them, scowling. He stood beside the driver's window peering in at them. Then he whipped off his glasses and bunched his fist.

'I know you!' he shouted pointing at Sam. 'You're the same damn people—'

'GO!' screamed Greg.

Sam slammed his foot hard down on the accelerator and dragged the steering wheel hard round. The tyres spun and the smell of burning rubber was everywhere. There was a yell of rage from Merv and a loud curse. But by then they were swerving past and racing for the road.

Twenty-one

Kyrek listened to the other crocodile approaching and ground his teeth in rage. A large male was swimming upstream looking for him, listening for him, calling him out. An aggressive younger male who was going to fight for this part of the river and everything that went with it. Power, food and control over the breeding grounds.

He had heard the first faint rumblings of the invader's approach while he was still half a mile away. Now the intruder's roaring sounded like rolling thunder. And getting closer with each thrust of his massive tail.

Kyrek knew what to expect. This would be his tenth challenger in the past four years. He could gauge his progress up river from the noise the birds were making. The crocodile swam into view and Kyrek grunted in alarm at his size.

The newcomer was swimming provocatively high on the surface of the river, his head, back and tail deliberately exposed to show his huge size. As he came nearer, he opened his jaws to show the waiting rows of wicked teeth. A huge V-shaped ripple spread away on either side of his massive head.

Now he was only fifty metres away and swimming fast. He slapped his head hard down on the water and thrashed his tail. He bellowed for a third time. Its meaning and ferocity were unmistakeable. Other challengers had not been as confident. Incensed, Kyrek moved out to meet him.

The two crocodiles drove straight at each other. They met head on with a thud that could be heard for hundreds of metres. They grappled at each other's jaws, fighting like dogs for purchase. A vicious see-sawing struggle began.

They reared up half out of the water, their teeth ripping and tearing and finally meshing together with bone-cracking force. The river boiled as they fought to wrap their tails round the other and rake open his soft underbelly with their claws.

They clutched each other in a cold, reptilian

embrace indifferent to pain, their unblinking eyes only centimetres apart. They wrestled in seething fury, seeking the momentary advantage which would let them seize the other's snout between their jaws and crush it into so much splintered, useless bone. Small waves broke along the banks.

Eventually, as if by mutual consent, they let go and circled each other, watching for a fresh opening. With a gigantic swirl the challenger swept in alongside Kyrek. Side by side the two of them lay facing in the same direction, their bodies almost touching. Then like a pair of synchronised swimmers, both males swung their heads outwards and with the extra momentum gained, crashed their heads together in a sickening thud.

There was no let-up, no respite. Every ten seconds their heads swung out and then came thudding together with pile-driving monotony. It became part of the morning. The watching birds grew bored and flew off.

And then quite suddenly, the thud-thudding stopped. One moment it was there, the next, it was all over. The contest had been decided. The challenger swam slowly away, his back and tail submerged. It was an admission of defeat. An acknowledgement of Kyrek's supremacy.

Kyrek watched until he was out of sight. He was almost asleep with exhaustion. He felt no emotion towards the other crocodile. He had survived and that was all that mattered. But there was still another challenger to be dealt with. A strange, silvery-coloured animal that roared defiance at him and left a bubbling track in its wake.

Twenty-two

'You're sure you've seen them before?' Coyle demanded. He tilted back in his chair and put both feet on top of the battered desk.

Danny flung out his arms. 'I'd recognize them anywhere. A black fellow and two teenagers. Merv and I found them snooping round the van bringing up the rabbits. Remember? They tried to get the doors open.'

Coyle frowned. 'Tell me where this was again?'

'Out on the highway. Close to here.'

'And you're certain they're the same people?'

Danny became even more agitated. 'Of course I am!' he shouted. 'Do you think I'm stupid or something?'

Coyle gave a little shrug. 'Don't sound much

like the heavy mob to me.'

'It's just too much of a coincidence,' Danny snapped. He pulled out a toothpick from a top pocket and began probing. 'They must know something. I've got a bad feeling about them.'

Coyle got to his feet. 'I think you're getting this all out of proportion,' he said soothingly. 'They don't sound like any law enforcement agency I've ever heard of. And believe me, I know plenty.'

He came round the desk and put an arm round Danny's shoulders. 'Listen my friend,' he said, 'the worst they can be is environmentalists, animal lovers. You read about these crazies every day in the newspapers. So what the heck! There's only another day to go. Then it'll all be finished. So, no worries!'

Danny shook his head and looked unconvinced. 'I've got this bad feeling about them,' he repeated, stubbornly.

Coyle slid open a drawer in the desk. He took out a bottle and a couple of glasses. 'They're just some kids and a local Aborigine,' he said handing Danny a drink. 'Who are they going to tell? And what do they know? Nothing! This is a legitimate establishment for scientific research.'

Danny said nothing. He emptied his glass moodily.

'Put an extra guard on tonight if it makes you feel any better,' Coyle suggested.

Danny thought about this and nodded. 'I will. So what's the plan now?'

Coyle patted a pocket. 'We pay off the guards tomorrow, then we go. They've got a really nice bonus to keep 'em sweet.'

'And Dorrell? What happens to Dorrell?'

Coyle looked surprised. 'He comes with us of course.'

'Say he refuses?'

Coyle shook his head. 'He won't. There's a million dollar pay-off waiting for him back at headquarters.' He laughed and winked at Danny. 'Well that's what I'll be telling him. He'll come for that!'

'So how do we get rid of him?' Danny wanted to know.

'Couldn't be easier,' said Coyle, filling their glasses again. 'He's going to be the victim of a tragic boating accident. As soon as we're out of sight of land we tie his ankles together and lower him head first over the side. Ten minutes should be enough. Then we untie him and leave him floating for the sharks. Very sad!'

There was a knock on the door. Danny went over and opened it. Dorrell was waiting there. He smiled brightly looking from one to the other. 'Someone wanted to see me?' he asked.

Coyle did not bat an eyelid. He switched on a big smile and came towards Dorrell with his hand outstretched in greeting. 'Come in Ray,' he welcomed. 'We were just saying what a great job you've done here. And now we've got some really exciting news for you personally. So come on in!'

Twenty-three

'There's no one following!' Tom shouted, scanning the road behind them. 'I can see for miles. We're on our own.'

'Hallelujah!' Greg exclaimed blowing out his cheeks in relief. 'Hear that Sam?'

Sam nodded but said nothing. His eyes flicked to the temperature gauge and he groaned. 'She's blown again,' he cried.

'There's a track on the left,' Greg indicated. 'Let's take it.'

By the time they had pulled off the highway and bumped their way towards the river, steam was hissing out from under the bonnet. They stopped well out of sight of the road. Sam switched the engine off. 'Nothing we can do until she cools down,' he told them.

'Why don't I make some tea?' Tom suggested.

Greg nodded. 'Great idea.' He saw Sam staring at the ground. 'What you looking at Sam?'

Sam pointed. 'Fresh tracks,' he told them. 'There's been a truck along here already this morning. Let's take a look.'

They followed him down to the river. Sam took his trilby off and fanned himself with it. 'Someone's been here with a boat a lot of times. See where they've loaded it off a trailer?' He looked up at Greg. 'Where's there to go round here?'

Greg shrugged. 'Who cares? Let's get back and see how bad the radiator is.'

When they finished the tea, Sam wriggled underneath the vehicle. His legs stuck out like matchsticks. 'It's a big job,' he shouted. 'The weld's split all the way along.'

'Can you fix it?' Greg demanded.

Sam nodded. 'Yeah I think so. But it'll take time. I'll need the big jack.'

'OK,' said Greg. 'Tom!' he called. 'Give us a hand will you mate?'

The jack was stowed away under a seat and they had to unload a lot of stores to get at it. It was heavy and awkward to manoeuvre. When they eventually lifted it down, Tom trundled it round to the front and helped Sam position it. Then they jacked up the 4×4.

Sam crawled underneath and had another long look. Greg joined him. Tom lay on his stomach peering up at the radiator. 'It's bad all right,' Greg confirmed. 'You're sure you can do it Sam? We can always radio Dad for help.'

Sam snorted. 'And what you think he'll say?' he demanded, sounding quite put out. 'He'll say, "That's what Sam Minamurra's for. Tell him to get on with it!" '

Greg said nothing.

'We need both the spare batteries, the jump leads and all the welding gear,' Sam told him.

'Did you get that Tom?' Greg asked, turning his head to look at him. 'Start humping it out, will you?'

They placed the batteries on the ground and wired them together. Next, Sam connected the welding torch to a spare battery terminal and then clipped the remaining lead to a flange at the bottom of the radiator.

Sam pulled on a pair of goggles and grinned

at Tom. 'Take a sleep. A long one!' Then he disappeared underneath.

At midday, Tom opened a tin of corned beef and made another brew of tea. They stood round the tailboard talking quietly. 'It's coming along,' Sam told them. 'But long time still to go.'

'If you can't fix it by tea time,' Greg said slowly, 'then we might as well camp here for the night. Tom and me can make camp while you're underneath.'

Sam nodded agreement. 'You're right. It'd be crazy to load all the gear back in the truck then take it back out again an hour later.'

When they had finished putting up the tent, Tom dragged out a bag of potatoes. 'Frying tonight,' he told Greg.

'I'll give you a hand,' Greg volunteered.

They sat at the foot of a tree and began peeling. 'Those people back there,' Tom said after a pause. 'Pretty scary weren't they? Especially the big one with the sunglasses.'

Greg nodded and shifted his chewing gum. 'Yeah,' he agreed. 'Something stinks about that whole set-up.' He shook his head. 'I mean look what happened this morning. That guy on the gate couldn't give a damn. We could be roasting in the middle of nowhere for all he cared. Up here that's sheer criminal behaviour!'

'What about those other men?' put in Tom eagerly. 'The little man with the funny ear. He gives me the creeps I can tell you.'

Greg nodded. 'Remember that business with the van? The driver? Remember how he held that knife? He sure knew how to use that all right. I'm glad I told Dad all about it.'

'They were pretty cruel the way they left all those animals shut up with no air.'

'Sam said they were rabbits,' Greg reflected. 'Lot of people wouldn't get too upset about that though. They're only vermin.'

'Well, if you want my opinion,' said Tom, 'I think they're doing experiments on them.'

'On rabbits?' Greg sounded sceptical.

'Why not? The big cigarette companies have used beagle puppies to experiment on for years. They still do,' Tom told him. 'They make them inhale smoke twenty-four hours a day to test out tar levels until they get lung cancer.'

Greg looked shocked. 'What the heck for?' he demanded.

'So they can cut them open and see how harmful

the tobacco would be on humans.'

'We had a beagle once,' Greg said thoughtfully. 'We called him Olly. Great little dog.' He looked at Tom with a scowl. 'So why don't they use rats?'

'Because years ago their scientists discovered that a beagle's lungs were the nearest things in nature to human lungs. You get the same things happening with other species,' Tom explained. 'It's just like organ transplants today. A pig's kidneys are identical to ours. That's why we're cloning them.'

'How do you know all this?' Greg asked.

'My dad's a vet,' Tom said simply. 'He told me all about it.'

Greg considered this for a while then said slowly, 'So that guy in the white coat . . .'

'Dorrell, the guard said his name was.'

'Right! Him. Do you think he's doing experiments?'

Tom nodded. 'Could be. He didn't look like a guard or anything, did he?'

'Hell's teeth!' Greg swore. 'You're right Tom. What was the place called? What did that sign on the road say?'

'Skinwatch? Something like that.'

Greg got to his feet. 'So all those buildings and things. Do you think that's what they're being used for?'

Tom looked at him blankly. 'Well yes. Probably.'

Greg swore and kicked the ground.

'But the place must be legal,' Tom argued. 'It's signposted and everything.'

Greg spat out his chewing gum. 'Maybe,' he said. 'But those men in there are bad.' He spelt the letters out. 'B-A-D.' He stared at Tom. 'I know that. You know that and Sam does for sure.' There was real anger in his voice. 'I've got an idea. I'm going to see how Sam's doing. Then I'm going for a walk. Want to come?'

'All right,' said Tom. 'How far we going?'

'About a mile. Bit more,' Greg told him. 'And then up there,' he said, pointing to some higher ground.

They walked in silence for half an hour. At the end of it, Tom felt like sagging. It was almost as hot as the sand dunes. Their feet kicked up a fine curtain of dust that hung round their knees. When they reached the foot of the hill they had a drink from their water bottles. Greg looked at Tom and said casually, 'From now on bang your feet down hard.'

'Why?' asked Tom, wondering if he really wanted to know.

'Helps scare away the snakes! Now, stick right behind me. And when we get near the top we're going to duck down and crawl the rest of the way. I don't want to be seen.'

'Who's going to see you out here?' Tom asked, mystified.

Greg grinned. 'The people in the research station for a start. It's just down the other side of this hill.'

Tom stared at him. 'You're joking! We're miles away. All that time on the road?'

Greg nodded. 'Yeah, I know! But take another look at the map. The road bends round quite a bit to miss the river. Anyway, let's go see. Oh! And from now on, no more talking.'

They threaded their way between large boulders and through waist-high scrub. Sharp thorns ripped at Tom's shirt. Just before they reached the crest, Greg made Tom lie down and wait while he wormed the last few metres forward on his stomach.

Tom stared at the ground in front of him and listened to the flies buzzing round his head. The earth was bright red and there were black ants

121

everywhere. He wondered what other things might be around.

He heard Greg give a low call. Gritting his teeth, Tom went forward to join him. The research station lay below them, no more than a few hundred metres away. The track they had driven along that morning was on the far side. Greg had brought a pair of binoculars with him. 'Looks like they're burning paper and stuff,' he whispered. 'Hey! There's the big man. What's he doing?'

He passed the glasses to Tom. As Tom took them, his elbow banged on a sharp piece of rock. He gasped at the sudden pain and the glasses slipped in his grasp.

'Watch it!' Greg hissed. 'Keep them out of the sun!' Tom bit his lip and put them carefully to his eyes.

But the flash they made had gone straight into Merv's eyes. Merv looked up, puzzled, watching for it to happen again. But it didn't. He scanned the hillside knowing it had come from somewhere up there. And then he realized it was no accident. With elaborate unconcern, he resumed dragging a bulging sack towards the incinerator.

Greg took the glasses again. 'Hey! That's great!'

he cried a moment later. 'There's a gully running behind the fence! That's just what I need.'

'What for?' whispered Tom.

'To sneak in, of course. I'm going to have a look around there tonight! And don't you dare go telling Sam. Understand?'

Twenty-four

An owl hooted and flew off into the darkness on silent wings. Greg sank to the ground on both knees and gulped in great draughts of air. He closed his eyes oblivious to everything except the pounding of his heart. He swayed from side to side, his chest heaving while he fought to get his breath back. Although the night was cool, he was covered in sweat. His hair was wet with it and his shirt clung to his body. He rubbed an arm over his face and head trying to mop it up.

He had come the long way round, carefully picking his way across the jumble of rocks at the bottom of the ridge. Now he had reached the gully. For the time being he would be safely out of sight of anyone in the research station.

The pain in his lungs eased. He peered at his watch. Almost midnight. Much later than he had anticipated. There was no way he'd make it back to the others on time. Poor old Sam! Greg smiled ruefully. He'd be going ballistic again.

He had found Greg trying to slip away unnoticed. 'You can't do this to me, Greg!' he had stormed. 'You get your stupid self caught . . . then what do I do here?' They had almost come to blows when Sam grabbed his arms and tried to hold him back.

But Greg knew he held the upper hand. There was no way Sam would leave Tom out on his own. He had promised Bob and Sarah that, back in Balgarri. Never mind, Greg thought. He'd make it up to him somehow. Now it was time to get moving.

Cautiously, he got to his feet and listened. There was nothing there to alarm him. The bottom of the gully was sandy and there was enough starlight to see quite well. He moved forward. After thirty paces or so it began to narrow and run uphill. He hunched his shoulders and moved slowly forward. The gully ended suddenly at the foot of a steep bank. Greg looked back along the way he had come. Nothing was following him.

He took a deep breath, reached as high as he

could and began hauling himself upwards. Just before the top he paused and carefully raised his head. He squinted into the glare of the overhead lights. He held his breath and waited. Nothing moved.

Reassured, he slid over the edge and lay hugging the ground. Immediately in front of him there was a low barbed-wire fence. Beyond it he could see slabs of light falling on the ground in front of open doors. Somewhere a radio was playing country and western music.

He froze suddenly as the figure of a man came out of one of the buildings and hurried across the compound. Greg thought it was Dorrell but he couldn't be certain. The man disappeared into another building. Moments later, Greg heard a door slam. He remained motionless for a while longer.

The fence was only waist high and made up of four strands of wire. It was not meant to form any real obstacle. He knelt in front of it and peeled off his denim jacket. He dropped it across the top strand and taking a deep breath, climbed over. He was in enemy territory!

He scuttled towards the nearest building and crouched down. It was all so different at night. And far more threatening than he had imagined.

He crept round the side of the building and found himself in a garage. The big jeep was parked there in an open bay. It looked squat and menacing. There were wooden packing cases nearby and what looked like a number of small refrigerators. An aluminium boat was parked up on chocks.

Greg sprinted across open ground, his shadow dancing in front of him. He flung himself down beside a rough concrete wall and waited. Nothing happened. He felt a sudden surge of elation. No one had seen him! There were no sudden shouts or the sound of footsteps running to investigate. There was only the noise of his own heart pumping.

On tiptoe, he sidled towards the door. There were lights on inside. The handle felt cold and sticky. Greg took a deep breath and pulled it open, just enough. Then he slipped inside.

It was a long room with overhead neon lights switched on at either end. The musky smell of animals was very strong. He closed the door behind him and stared around. He walked between the rows of cages peering in. In some of them, the rabbits paused from their feeding to stare. In others, they sat motionless with dead eyes. There were hundreds of them. Greg felt his skin crawl.

He crossed to a workbench and gazed at the complicated array of glass tubing and beakers. A pale, yellowish liquid was being distilled. It ran down thick glass tubing from a sealed machine mounted on the wall through a series of condensers to an ordinary-looking plastic bottle held in a clamp.

A red light in the machine started to glow. There was a loud click followed by the hum of a centrifuge starting up. Greg backed away. As he did so, he noticed a box painted fluorescent yellow under another bench. He stooped to investigate. To his surprise he found it was made of polystyrene. He pulled it out and took off the lid. Packed into individual compartments were two similar-sized bottles. There was room for eight more.

Greg's mind raced. He was not sure what he had stumbled on but he knew instinctively that there was something evil here. The silent stare of the rabbits bore testimony. It was time to get out. And fast. He turned to leave.

He was almost at the door when it was flung open. A huge shape filled the doorway. Greg tried to dodge past. There was a lot of shouting and a sudden blow that drove the air from his lungs. He fell in agony to the floor, clutching his stomach with both hands. Then all the lights snapped on and the triumphant figure of Merv stood towering over him, blocking the only way out.

Twenty-five

Tom woke with a start. He hadn't meant to fall asleep. He had been trying to comfort Sam after the dreadful row with Greg. Yes! He remembered now. He had come into the tent to get something. He must have lain down on his bed and nodded straight off.

He sat up guiltily and scrabbled round for the torch he kept under the pillow. Poor old Sam. He had been frantic with worry when Greg told him what he was going to do. In the end, Sam had got Greg to swear he'd be back by midnight.

Screening the torch with his hand, Tom flashed it round the tent. He shone it on Greg's bed. It was empty. With a sickening feeling he looked at his watch. It was almost one o'clock! Where the heck was Greg?

Tom slipped outside and looked up at the immensity of the Australian night sky. He felt totally insignificant and alone. In the distance, an animal shrieked. Or it might have been a bird. Greg was somewhere out there. Silently, Tom cursed Greg for his selfishness. What was he trying to prove?

A voice spoke quietly beside him and he bit his tongue in shock. 'Tom! I got to find him. Maybe he's hurt bad, bleeding somewhere! He said he'd be back long time ago. Tom! I'm worried sick for him!' Sam's voice ended in a sob.

A wave of sympathy engulfed Tom. He hesitated then awkwardly put his arm round the man's shoulders. He wanted desperately for Sam to find his old self-assurance again. And as he stood there feeling helpless and angry, he knew what they must do.

'You're right Sam! We've got to find Greg. But I'm coming with you. No! Please! Listen! You know I'll keep up. Besides, there's no way I'm staying here on my own.'

'Bob's going to go mad,' Sam moaned. 'You've never seen him angry . . .'

'Bob's never going to know,' Tom interrupted. 'I'm not going to tell him. And Greg never will.

131

Come on Sam! Don't argue. You're wasting time!'

Five minutes later, Tom was hurrying to keep up. Sam ran with his head on one side scanning the ground. At last they reached the gully. Sam dragged Tom down beside him.

'Greg's been here,' Sam whispered. 'See!' He pointed at the ground. Then without waiting, he ran along the gully bent double. Tom followed panting hard. Sam found the place where Greg had crossed the wire. He helped Tom up then lay beside him staring into the compound.

'I'm going after him,' Sam breathed in his ear.

'Wait,' Tom hissed, grabbing his wrist. 'Listen!'

There were sounds of voices and someone shouting. Doors slammed. Then a searchlight came on. Its beam swinging towards them.

Twenty-six

Merv dragged Greg into Coyle's office and flung him down in front of the desk.

'What the hell!' shouted Coyle, knocking over his chair as he leapt to his feet.

'Found him snooping around,' Merv explained with relish.

Coyle looked at him for a long moment then nodded. 'You were right Merv! Hell's teeth!' He came round the desk and prodded Greg with his shoe. 'Where did you find him?'

'Main hut,' Merv told him. 'Hanging round the distillation plant.'

Coyle swore. 'What's the damage?' he demanded, as Dorrell came rushing in.

'Looks OK. I don't think anything's been touched.'

'Got him just in time then, didn't I?' said Merv with a grin.

Coyle swore again. 'Stick him in that chair!' he ordered and watched as Merv reached down and yanked Greg upright. Then he kicked the boy's legs from under him and dropped him down on to a hard-backed chair.

Coyle pointed at Dorrell. 'Get Danny,' he ordered. 'Then do a proper check of the lab. Report back here in twenty minutes.' He nodded to Merv. 'It's time we had a little chat with our new friend here. So Merv, will you start?'

Merv grinned. His hand reached out and twisted his fingers into Greg's hair. The boy yelled.

'Who sent you?' Coyle demanded. 'And where're your mates? The black fellow and the other kid.'

Merv tightened his grasp and started to lift Greg up bodily by the hair. The boy screamed and tore at Merv's hand. The man held him upright for five more seconds then let go.

Greg fell back clutching his head and moaning. He had never felt such pain before. His scalp was literally being ripped off.

'What's your name?' demanded Coyle.

Through the tears Greg told him.

'Who sent you? Was it the police?'

'No,' Greg sobbed, 'but they know all about you.'

Coyle's eyes widened. He made a gesture with his hand. Merv stepped forward and slapped Greg twice in the face. Greg slumped to one side. Merv bunched his hand in the front of his jacket and sat him upright again.

There was blood in Greg's mouth. A lot of it and all his teeth felt loose. His face was quite numb. He looked across at Coyle's bland expression and guessed the man was a killer.

'So what's your interest in this place, then?' Coyle demanded.

'The van,' Greg mumbled. 'And Sam getting beaten up. I told my dad all about it. He told the police in Darwin. He's got a friend there.' He looked round and saw that the little man with the funny ear had come in.

Greg pointed to him. 'We saw him today when our truck needed fixing. We had to stop by the river. So I went up the hill to have a look. I just wanted to know what you were doing. That's all. I promise!'

Merv moved towards him but Coyle held up a hand. 'Where's the rest of them?'

'By the river,' Greg said. 'Couple of miles away.

135

No one knows I'm here,' Greg lied. 'They're sleeping.' He stopped, knowing he had said too much. Now the others were in danger too. Sweat poured down his face.

Coyle drummed his fingers on the desk and studied Greg. Dorrell came back. 'Everything's fine,' he said.

'Can I use my knife?' Danny asked with a smile.

'Look at me Greg,' Coyle commanded.

Greg did so. He could feel his legs shaking. He was fighting not to show how terrified he felt. He stared back at Coyle as defiantly as he could.

'You're sure you're telling me the truth?'

Greg nodded.

Coyle thought for a moment. 'Lock him up in the gatehouse,' he ordered. 'I'll decide what to do with him later.'

In a dream, Greg felt himself being dragged out into the night air. He kept stumbling and falling over his feet. But that wasn't important. The only thing that mattered now was what happened to Sam and Tom.

Twenty-seven

Tom and Sam lay motionless behind the wire fence. Every light had now been turned on inside the compound. Men came pouring out of one of the buildings. Horrified they watched Greg being dragged away. His hands were tied behind his back. Merv was holding him by the arm and hustling him along.

'They're taking him to the gatehouse,' whispered Tom.

They saw Merv and Greg disappear inside. Moments later, Merv came back out slamming the door behind him. They watched him walk down the slope towards them and lay rigid until they heard Danny calling. Merv turned and went into another hut.

Sam nudged Tom. He jerked a thumb over his shoulder at the sky. 'We got to go! Dawn's coming up soon,' he said in a low voice. 'It'll be light in half an hour.'

Tom did not respond. He was picturing the gatehouse in his memory. He remembered there were some bushes close by. And this same low barbed-wire fence.

'Wait ....' he whispered.

'Tom!' Sam was tugging at his arm. 'We got to get back and radio Bob Bradley for help. What you hanging around for?'

'It's Greg!' Tom hissed back. 'We've got to tell him we know. That we're getting help. We must! He'll be going mad. Then we make contact ...'

Sam punched the ground in frustration. 'No! That's crazy talk. If we get caught then we're all in trouble! These guys don't mess around! Let me think ...'

He squinted into the lights, following the fence round towards the gatehouse. Ten minutes, he thought. Longer, if there were any gullies to cross. They would have to move very fast. Luckily, the men all seemed busy inside the compound itself.

'OK,' he whispered and slithered back into the

gully. 'You stay right behind me. Understand?' And without looking back, he set off at a run.

They kept to the darkness and skirted the fence. After an eternity, they reached the bushes beside the gatehouse and crouched down. The front of the building was bathed in brilliant light. The door was only ten metres away. But was it locked?

There were men's voices everywhere. They could hear boxes being moved and the smashing of glass. Sam touched him lightly on the shoulder. He beckoned Tom to follow. The back of the gatehouse was in darkness but Sam's sharp eyes had seen something. There was a small window high overhead. It was not quite closed.

For a moment they stood staring up at it. Then Sam dropped to his knees. 'Get up on my shoulders,' he urged. Tom put his arm through the window and found the metal catch. He pushed down hard. It did not move. Angrily, he hit it with the side of his fist, oblivious to the pain. A couple more blows and then it was swinging open.

'Can you get through?' Sam called.

Tom licked his lips. It was a very small opening. He squeezed his legs through and wondered whether his shoulders would fit. Visions of Merv finding him hanging there unable to move flashed through his mind.

He fell with a crash on to a lavatory bowl and went sprawling. He struggled to his feet. Then he was up and out of the cubicle into a dimly-lit corridor. 'Greg! Greg!' he cried.

There were two closed doors ahead of him. He heard a groan and Greg's voice. The door was locked. Tom looked round. There was no sign of a key. 'Watch out!' he called and took a run at the door. His foot hit the panel below the lock. The wood splintered. The noise was terrible. But the lock held. Tom thought he heard a shout outside.

Tom ran at it again. His leading foot hit the lock square on. There was a loud bang and the door flew open.

Greg was on his feet, swaying from side to side and grinning lop-sidedly. 'Tom! Brilliant—' he started to say.

'Quick!' Tom screamed at him. And then he realized there was no way Greg could get through the little window. The front door was their only way out. What happened if it was locked? He was suddenly drenched in sweat. There were more shouts. Louder this time. And the sound of pounding feet.

They raced back along the passage. Someone was rattling the door handle. He heard a key turn. The door was flung open. Tom gave a little moan. Merv loomed up, his hands reaching out to grab him. Beside him, Greg put his head down and ran at the man's stomach.

Somehow Tom slipped past. He dodged under the barrier and was aware of Sam running beside him. He could hear Greg yelling and behind him the ugly roar of voices. Then the two of them were fleeing into the welcoming darkness.

Coyle watched them go and knew his men would not catch them. But he was good in a crisis. He always had been. By the time Danny and the others had given up the chase, he had his temper firmly back under control.

The men gathered round him, their chests heaving. Coyle knew what must be done. 'Merv!' he ordered. 'Leave now! Find their camp. They've got a vehicle there. It'll have a radio. Put it out of action. And get rid of the truck. Make it look like an accident. Then get back on the highway and patrol it. They won't get far!'

He turned to Danny. 'Get the boat trailer hitched up. Take Dorrell and this damn boy out to the *Bluewater*. Then come back here for me. Fast! Really fast. Got that? I want to be out of here by midday at the latest!'

Finally, he looked over at Greg and walked towards him. He slipped a hand under the boy's arm and led him away to one side. 'See that sun rising?' he asked conversationally. Greg looked nonplussed. 'Enjoy!' said Coyle pushing his face into Greg's. 'Because it's going to be the last damn one you're ever going to see!'

Twenty-eight

'We've got to get help,' Sam gasped. 'Right now!'

Tom barely heard him. He lay sprawled on the ground where he had fallen, his legs buckling under him, unable to take another step. Dimly, he heard Sam shouting his name then felt himself being shaken by the shoulders. All Tom wanted to do was sleep. Nothing else mattered. Not the men who had chased them. Not even Greg ... Greg! What had happened to him?

He opened his eyes and struggled up into a sitting position. Sam was bending over him, his face grey with worry. 'Tom!' he pleaded. 'Come on Tom. Otherwise Greg will die!'

Tom stared at him. 'Die?' he muttered. 'What do you mean die?'

'Those men are going to kill him. I know they are. We've got to get help.'

It was getting light and the sky over the far horizon was a brilliant orange. Tom stared round but all he could see were the same dried-up gum trees and spindly clumps of grass.

'Help?' he asked. 'Where're we going to get help from out here?'

'The radio!' Sam shouted. 'On the truck. Remember!'

Tom did. Painfully, he got to his feet and grinned. 'Fantastic! I'd forgotten. How long before the police get here?'

Sam waved his arms impatiently. 'An hour. Longer maybe ... Depends ...' and he looked meaningfully at Tom.

The boy's smile faded. He blinked and choked down the cry of protest that was already rising in his throat. Every muscle in his body groaned in protest.

'Make me proud of you, Tom!' Sam said quietly, and looked away. 'You ready?' he asked a few moments later. Tom took a deep breath and brushed past him in a shambling run.

The sun was high when they reached the river. 'Not far now,' Sam reassured him. 'You're doing great.' A hundred metres further on he suddenly stopped and sniffed at the air. He made a face.

'What's wrong?' Tom gasped.

'Car exhaust,' Sam told him. 'You stay here. I'll take a look.'

Tom flopped down without a word and lay on his back in the dust. It felt more comfortable than any bed he had ever slept in. Sam was back in a matter of minutes, dragging his feet and looking utterly crushed.

Tom looked up at him and his heart sank. 'What's up? What's happened?'

Sam sat down and held his head in both hands. His shoulders heaved. With a dreadful premonition Tom struggled up and knelt beside him. 'Sam! Tell me! Please!'

'They've taken Greg away,' Sam muttered. 'We'll never find him now.' And then in despair cried, 'Greg's my friend. A son to me.'

'Where's he gone? How do you know?'

Sam groaned. 'They dragged him into a boat . . . And I let him go poking round that place . . .' He knuckled his eyes. 'The men got here first. They've trashed the radio. Come and look.'

The 4×4 lay at a steep angle, its rear wheels just

above the surface of the river. The current made a slight furrow on either side of the steering wheel. Tom stared at it in silence. The enormity of it all slowly sinking in. 'So what happened?' he asked in a low voice.

Sam pointed at some tyre marks. 'That black jeep's been here. See how it rubs out all the other tracks? It's a lot heavier. Then others came to launch their boat. See these scrapes? And these are Greg's boot marks!'

Tom stared at the ground not knowing what to say or do. Eventually he asked, 'What about the tent?'

'They left that alone.'

'So what do we do now?' Tom asked. But Sam did not reply.

'I know!' cried Tom triumphantly. 'Why don't we go back to the road and stop the first vehicle that comes along?'

Sam shook his head. 'No one lives round here. Not for miles and miles. Only person coming by'll probably be Merv. He'll be watching for us.'

Tom's shoulders sagged.

Sam watched the river flowing past. A branch swung lazily in the current. A scarlet butterfly landed on it and spread its wings. He wondered how long the branch would take to reach the Sound. It was only a few miles from here through the mangroves. The men would have gone that way as well. There was nowhere upstream for them to go.

Beyond the Sound was the ocean. The men would need a proper sea-going boat if that's where they were heading. Sam frowned. His family were fishing folk. They had lived along the Sound for generations. They would know every boat anchored there.

And there was another thing. What a fool he was. Of course! They had a radio set there too. The government had installed it only a few months ago. He gave a loud whoop and danced a little jig. He swung round to tell Tom the good news and the cry died away on his lips.

The boy was staring at him as if he had gone mad. Perhaps he had. Which was just as well. Because to reach his family in time, he was going to have to find a way through the swamp. There was no other choice. To go around the swamp would take a whole day.

But if he got lost in the mangroves, then Greg's chances of survival would be nil. And Tom's not much better. Sam's brain reeled. But there was no other choice.

'Tom!' he said in a strong voice. 'You're a great mate. You've got real guts. But you've got to be ten times braver than you've ever been before.' Tom stared at him and felt his heart sink.

'If I take a short cut through the swamp I could be on the radio by midday calling up the police. If I leave now I might just be in time to help Greg.' He put out his hand and grasped Tom's arm. 'But it means you've got to stay here on your own for the next twelve hours.'

'But why can't I come with you? I'll keep up. You know I can!'

'You ever been in mangroves before?' Sam challenged. 'Got many swamps in your country?' Then seeing the hurt in Tom's face, he said, 'Look, Tom! The mangroves terrify me. I get nightmares about them. If you fall in we'll waste a whole lot of time. Besides, I may not be able to pull you out.'

He put both hands on the boy's shoulders. 'Greg needs every second there is. When I get to my village, I'll call the police right away to come and fetch you. Trust me.'

'But there must be somewhere nearer we can go for help?' Tom pleaded.

Sam shook his head. 'Nearest town's four hours'

drive by truck. And we don't have one any more. Remember?'

Tom nodded miserably. Sam tried to grin but failed. 'Stay in the tent and get some sleep. You'll be OK. You're smart,' and he put his hand out. It felt odd shaking hands in the middle of nowhere. But Tom was grateful Sam had done it. It made him feel that they were equals somehow in the fight to save Greg.

Sam had one parting piece of advice. 'Keep away from the river! Just keep right away!' Then he was gone, running easily with an energy Tom could only marvel at. He watched him slip between the trees and disappear. He stood motionless staring after him. The sun grew hotter and the buzz of insects filled his head. For the very first time in his life, Tom was totally alone.

Twenty-nine

The cabin was small and gloomy. It smelt of diesel and old fish. Greg dragged himself across the floor to the cabin wall. He sat up against it then levered himself upright. When he got to his feet he closed his eyes and felt sick again.

His head ached from the beating Merv had given him. The pain in his wrists and arms was intense. The men had lashed his hands behind his back with nylon cords. Danny had laughed when Greg had asked to be untied.

'Listen to me,' Danny had told him at the entrance to the cabin. 'In a couple of hours you'll wish it was only your hands you had to worry about!' Then he had given Greg a shove that sent the boy sprawling.

Greg heard the key turn in the lock and the noise

of Danny going back up on deck. A few minutes later, the outboard engine started. Greg listened to it fading away until there was only the sound of his own heart thumping and the slap of waves against the *Bluewater*'s hull.

And all the time a terrible dread was growing inside him. Coyle's threat rang in Greg's ears like some great bell. Were they really going to kill him? Some time later today? When they all came back on board? No! It was crazy. It had to be. They were trying to frighten him. This was television drama not real life. His natural optimism tried its best to reassure him.

But in that case, he thought, why was he locked up in this filthy little cabin? A prisoner. They had kidnapped him. They could go to prison for this. So they must mean business. This was for real after all! And no one even knew where he was! No one!

He thought of his parents and Sam too. A wave of misery broke over him. Afterwards, he felt a little better.

The only light in the cabin filtered in through a small porthole. It was stained with salt and there was a fresh seagull dropping down one side. Greg peered out. The wind was getting up. He could see

151

some wave tops foaming white. He thought he could see huts in between the palm trees along the shore. Those people were so close. They'd be bound to know Sam's family.

He wondered what had happened to Sam and to Tom as well. That was a really gutsy thing they had done trying to rescue him. They must have got away. So perhaps there was some tiny bit of hope for him after all? Good old Sam and Tom, of course. They wouldn't let him down. He was sure of that. There must be some way out of this.

He thought he could hear a man singing. He put his head on one side and listened intently. Yes. There it was again. It must be Dorrell. The man was singing at the top of his voice. He sounded very happy.

Greg hadn't paid much attention to Dorrell on the way here in the dinghy. He had been far too frightened and confused. Now he racked his brain trying to remember more about him.

Yes! He was the man in the white coat and he did seem different from the others. For a start he was not as violent! It wasn't much to go on but it was better than nothing. Dorrell might be his only hope. And there wasn't much time left.

He took a deep breath and yelled, 'Dorrell! Dorrell! Dorrell!' He drummed his heels on the cabin floor. 'Dorrell! Dorrell! Dorrell!'

Thirty

Some instinct made Sam hesitate. He looked up and saw the snake less than a metre away. It lay along the branch in front of him. The snake's tongue flickered as its head swung towards his outstretched hand.

Sam jerked it away and lost his balance. His bare feet slipped on the mangrove's twisted root. He yelled in fear as he teetered above the grey, stinking mud fifty centimetres below him. Mud that would suck him down into oblivion and close gently over his head.

Frantically, he windmilled his arms. He saw the snake glide upwards into the leaves above him. He fell forward grabbing at the branch and hanging on to it with all his strength. He cursed himself for becoming overconfident. Up until now, he had weaved his way through the gloom with a skill few could equal.

He had kicked off his worn trainers a long way back. His bare feet gripped the mangrove bark far better. He could balance safely just long enough before leaping to the next root. But he had failed to see the snake until it was almost too late.

There were experienced men who had fallen and been drowned in the slime. Men paralysed by snake bite; some driven mad by the mosquitoes and others by the terrible knowledge that they were lost. He had known some of them.

Sam shook his head. He had to get on. There was no way back for him now. He had come too far. His instincts were his only guide. He knew the river was close by. He could picture it blue and sparkling in the sunshine. But the beauty of the river was deceptive. In reality it was a death trap. Saltwater crocodiles and sharks infested its brackish waters. Sea snakes lay on the surface enjoying the warmth.

He thought he was still a good mile from the village. His great dread was finding an open stretch of water in front of him. A diversion took up time. And time was one thing he did not have.

The sound of the approaching engine took some

time to register in Sam's mind. At first it was part of the swaying cloud of vicious biting mosquitoes that covered his face and every bit of exposed skin.

Sam jumped across the mangroves as quickly as he dared towards the sound. He reached the river just as a silver-coloured boat swept past, its bow high out of the water and a rush of water sluicing along its sides. It was the men's boat returning up river. Sam recognized the man in the stern. The small one with the funny ear. Danny. But where was Greg? He watched the boat speed past. They had dropped Greg off somewhere and he had a growing certainty he knew where.

The wash came splashing up over his legs. It felt wonderful. Sam took a deep breath and turned back into the swamp. The mangroves closed in all around him.

Thirty-one

Tom opened his eyes reluctantly. Something had woken him. He lay gazing at the tent roof wondering where he was. The delicious languor of sleep pulled at his eyelids. He closed them and immediately felt himself slipping away . . .

The screams of a pair of squabbling crows brought him upright. They were just outside the tent. He yawned. Why was he lying on his bed in the middle of the day? He couldn't even remember going to sleep. 'Sam!' he called. And then his memory came cartwheeling back.

He scrambled up and rushed outside. The crows screeched in surprise and took off with a loud flapping of wings. He watched their shapes distorting in the heat haze. Tom looked at his watch.

Ten o'clock. Sam had been gone over four hours. How far had he got? Perhaps he had reached his village by now. The police might already be on their way.

Another thought struck him. What if he hadn't got there? What if he was lying injured or lost? Tom thrust the thought away. He must never ever think like that. His mouth had gone dry at the thought. He went back into the tent, found a water container and drank what was left. The water was warm and flat and not at all refreshing. He remembered there was a lot more in their vehicle. An ice box too with some cans left over.

He also remembered Sam's warning and decided to wait for another hour. The police might be here by then. He rummaged around in the tent looking for something to eat and found a half-eaten apple under Greg's bed. It was covered with ants. He threw it out of the tent.

Next, he played a game tossing pebbles at the old water container until he became bored. He looked at his watch again and couldn't believe only eight minutes had gone by. This was awful. He was also much thirstier.

He stood up, collected the empty water bottle

and after a lot of hesitation, headed for the river. He remembered Greg's advice and stamped his feet as he walked. Some minutes later, he recognized the screen of bushes on top of the river bank.

He pushed through and then stopped in horror. A Land Rover was parked there facing him less than ten metres away. The men must have returned while he had been asleep. He had heard nothing! His legs began to tremble. He wanted to turn and run for it but he was rooted to the spot. Like a rabbit in headlights, he stared helplessly at the windscreen, waiting to be discovered.

But no one shouted in surprise or triumph. There was no movement at all inside. Slowly it dawned on him that there was no one there. He waited, hardly daring to breathe, straining his senses for any sign of the men. A twig snapping underfoot; a bird shrilling in alarm or even the smell of a cigarette. But none came.

Holding his breath, he circled the vehicle. With his heart thumping madly, he came round the back. But there was no one hiding there waiting to leap out at him. He gave a long gasp of relief. At the driver's door he paused. An idea, a brilliant idea, had him tugging open the door and sliding inside.

His fingers felt for the ignition key. He bent to look and saw it was not there.

Furiously he searched along the dashboard, then in the door pockets. Nothing!

He banged at the wheel in rage. Everything ruined just because of one little piece of metal!

He looked down again and noticed the radio tucked away below the dashboard.

With a trembling hand he switched it on. A green light glowed. Tom pressed the transmission switch down. The green light flickered and he heard the hiss of static. It was working! The radio was working! This was even better! He could get help right away. His spirits soared.

Tom closed his eyes in concentration, pressed the switch and broadcast. 'This is Tom for Balgarri Downs. Come in please ...' He swallowed and waited for a moment then repeated the message. 'Come in please, Balgarri Downs. This is Tom. Come in ... it's urgent!'

He made the call several more times with growing impatience. What was wrong? Why was no one answering? He called again and stared at the radio feeling baffled. It was letting them all down. He had been banking on it. And then someone answered!

It was a man's voice. He sounded hesitant and unfamiliar with the procedures.

'This is fishing boat *Bluewater*. Is that you, base?' the voice asked.

Tom's eyes bulged. It was the men! He was talking to one of the men! Of course! How stupid could he be? The men would have set the radio to their own frequency. They'd all have heard him. Now Greg would be in even more danger. All because of his stupidity.

With a cry of despair, Tom spun the frequency dial as hard as he could to get away from the man's voice. There was more static and Tom realized with a sinking heart that his mind had gone a total blank. He could not remember the police frequency or his uncle's. There was nothing he could do to help anyone. Not Greg, not Sam, not even himself. He was a total failure.

Someone had taped a strip of paper on the dashboard. He stared at it uncomprehendingly. He just wanted to die. Then like a holograph the jumble of letters slowly began to form a recognizable word.

It read 'Flying Doctor 4774 mHz'. In a dream, he spun the dial again. There were voices! Women's voices. He cut in ... 'Hello Flying Doctor. Please help me. My name's Tom Woods. My uncle is Bob Bradley. They've taken Greg prisoner. Sam's gone for help to his village . . .'

He broke off. He could hear the noise of an engine approaching. There was no response from the radio. Frantically he repeated the message. A woman's voice answered. She sounded puzzled.

'Hello?' she said. 'This is the Flying Doctor. Is someone sick?'

The engine noise was much louder. It was an outboard. The boat must be about to beach. There were only seconds left. 'Tell Uncle Bob to hurry,' he shouted into the microphone. 'The men are coming back. They're from the research place near the river. Hurry!'

He dropped the microphone and swung his legs out of the door. A man was coming through the bushes towards him. The little man with the misshapen ear. He saw the man's mouth open in a shout. His hand went to his waist belt. Then Tom was skidding round the back of the Land Rover and running for his life.

Thirty-two

Sam could smell the sea and knew he was almost
there. The mangroves ended abruptly and he
stepped out on to firm white sand. The glare was
overpowering. He had to shield his eyes to see. Tall
palm trees nodded gracefully. Hermit crabs scuttled
away in front of him. There were fishing boats pulled
up on the beach. The sun shone on waves whipped
up by a strong breeze. It was a new world.

He gave a yell of triumph. He had got through.
On impulse, he ran into the sea and dived head first
into a wave. Nothing had ever felt as wonderful. It
swept away the mosquitoes and all the filth and
sweat.

He let the waves tumble him over, then turned to
wade back to the shore. He was no longer alone. A

small crowd of children were laughing and pointing at him. His eldest brother Winyara was running through the palm trees towards him. There was a noisy, happy reunion.

For a few minutes Sam could not make himself heard. He looked back at the sea half expecting to see the men's dinghy returning. He threw his hands up and shouted for them all to be quiet.

They looked at his face and saw something was wrong. He had come here on foot. Through the swamp. Silence fell. Sam looked at Winyara who was the head of the family. 'I need to use the radio,' Sam told him. 'It's life or death.'

Their eyes widened. 'I've got a mate in big danger. Young Greg, my boss's son. He's a prisoner on a boat out there somewhere. I've got to talk with the police. Urgent . . .' his voice died away.

Winyara was shaking his head. The others looked away and shuffled their feet. Sam stared round at them. 'What's the problem?' he shouted.

'Sorry Sam!' his brother replied quietly. 'The radio's bust. It's useless. We had a bad electrical storm up here seven days ago. The set got hit by lightning. We're waiting for the government fellow to come and replace it.' He looked wretched. 'Sorry,

Sam. We can't help you!' Winyara held his hands out in apology.

Sam gaped at him. 'You're joking. You've got to be! Got to be . . .' his voice trailed away. His eyes filled with the bitter tears of failure. He turned his back on them, gazing out over the Sound. 'There's got to be a way!'

Winyara led him down towards the sea. 'I was out fishing this morning,' he said gravely. 'Tell me about this boat you think the boy is on.'

Thirty-three

Someone was thumping on the deck overhead. Greg renewed his efforts. 'Dorrell! Dorrell! Dorrell!' he shouted. He coughed. His throat was getting sore. He heard a man's voice complaining and the sound of feet thudding down the steps outside.

A key rattled in the lock and the door was flung open. Dorrell stood there. He peered into the cabin. 'What the heck do you want?' he demanded thickly. He swayed and put out a hand on either side of him. He smelt strongly of drink.

Greg had not bargained for this. His mind raced, wondering how best to approach him. 'Sorry to bother you Mr Dorrell,' he said very politely, 'but can I please ask you a favour?'

Dorrell stared at him and frowned in

concentration. 'What's up then?'

Greg tried to look apologetic. 'It's my arms,' he explained. 'I'll get gangrene in them if you don't cut me out of these ropes. They're killing me.'

Dorrell blinked. 'Know something?' he confided. 'I feel sorry for you being mixed up in all this.' He looked over his shoulder and added, 'But don't tell the others I said that, will you?'

'Of course not!' promised Greg.

Dorrell grinned at him. 'Thanks. Just had a shark snooping round the back end,' he confided. 'Threw a bottle at it.'

'Did you hit it?'

Dorrell chuckled. 'No. Got close though. Can you swim?' he asked suddenly.

'No,' Greg lied.

'So you'll stay put on the boat then?'

Greg nodded. 'You bet.'

'OK,' said Dorrell. 'Tell you what I'll do. Seeing you can't go far and the others will be back soon, I'll cut you free but I'll tie one of your legs to the rail first. How does that grab you?'

Greg took a deep breath to hide his elation. He couldn't trust himself to speak. Instead he nodded vigorously and let Dorrell propel him up the short ladder, through a roomy wheelhouse and out on to the deck. Dorrell rummaged round and found a short length of rope. Then he bent down and began lashing Greg to the guardrail.

Greg looked down at the man's head. He had a sudden overwhelming desire to kick Dorrell as hard as he could. He shut his eyes and fought the urge down. Doing that would achieve nothing. As long as his hands were tied he was helpless.

'Turn round!' Dorrell ordered. Greg had a glimpse of a long curved knife. He tensed wondering what it would feel like to be stabbed. But Dorrell was as good as his word. He sawed through the ropes and then stood back. 'It may hurt a bit,' he warned.

It did! Greg danced in pain, shouting and cursing and flapping his arms as the blood returned. He made no attempt to be brave. When at last it was over, he sagged against the rail and was sick over the side.

'Have a beer!' Dorrell thrust an opened can at him. Greg drank it greedily. Dorrell was clutching a bottle and taking swigs from it with evident enjoyment. He gave Greg a friendly wave and disappeared below.

Greg took stock. The boat was close to twenty metres long and roomy. Behind the wheelhouse there was a pile of fishing nets. There was rust everywhere. The wind was strengthening. He could feel the *Bluewater* tugging at the anchor chain and stubbing her bows into passing waves as if impatient to be under way.

He looked at the shore and for a moment his heart raced. A boat had appeared. But it wasn't the men. This boat was much longer and darker in colour. He breathed a huge sigh of relief. He tested the knots holding him. They were tight. Dorrell had done a good job. Perhaps he was a sailor in his spare time.

'Learnt to do them at university,' Dorrell told Greg, coming back on deck. 'So leave off mate or you'll go back down. Anyway,' he confided, 'the others'll be here soon. So . . . enjoy!'

He waved the bottle at Greg and perched on the captain's stool. He tipped the bottle up and drank.

'What's going to happen to me?' asked Greg.

Dorrell didn't seem to hear him. Greg shouted the question again. Dorrell made a face. 'Don't ask me. What do I know? I'm only a ruddy scientist.'

Greg considered. 'Were you experimenting on all those rabbits?' he asked.

Dorrell nodded. 'Yeah. Lots and lots of poor little bunnies. Stupid things.' He made a face and drank some more. He yawned and sat with his eyes closed, rocking with the motion of the boat.

'I thought scientists only used rats.' Greg sounded dubious. 'What did you need rabbits for? Sounds crazy to me.'

Dorrell's eyes opened wide. He swung round in his chair. 'Listen mate,' he was suddenly aggressive, 'you ever heard of the pituitary gland?' Greg had. It was something Tom had talked about.

'It's the body's master gland or something,' he told the man.

Dorrell nodded. 'Right! And do you know what its function is?'

Greg shook his head. 'I've forgotten.'

'It stimulates growth. It's the body's power house,' Dorrell told him. 'And I'm the guy who's made the big discovery.' He beamed at Greg who looked blank. 'I found out a couple of years ago,' Dorrell went on, 'that some of the hormones you find inside a rabbit's pituitary can be processed to produce one hell of a reaction in humans.'

Greg was concentrating as hard as he could. 'How big a reaction?'

Dorrell blew out his cheeks. 'I call it rocket fuel,' he said. 'I've been working on it for six years. Put a couple of drops in a town's water supply and they'll be dancing in the streets. Like a swig?' He thrust the bottle towards Greg.

'What is it?'

'White rum. Beauty on a day like this.'

'Too strong for me,' Greg told him. He looked past the man and saw the strange boat was nearer, much nearer. He also noticed it was crammed with people. It seemed to be heading in their direction but it was hard to tell. It was low in the water and frequently hidden by the waves.

If it got really close he could shout for help. Yes! If he made a scene they were bound to come close to see what all the fuss was about. They might even know Sam's name. Perhaps he could persuade them to release him. It was a long shot but the flicker of hope began to grow again.

'Where the heck are the others?' Dorrell grumbled. He held a wrist out in front of him using his other hand to steady it. 'What's the time?' he demanded.

'I've lost my watch,' Greg told him, then joked, 'perhaps they've gone a different way and left you.'

It didn't go down at all well. Dorrell scowled and slipped heavily off the stool. Greg saw that he had drunk most of the bottle.

'Look kid!' he said slowly. 'I'm the brains of this organization. It's my show. Understand?' He staggered back against the instrument console as a larger wave than usual burst against the bow.

'They need me. Boss man told me that yesterday. "Dorrell," he said, "you're the boy for us. How does a million-dollar bonus grab you?"' He caught a dribble of rum from the corner of his mouth and wiped it on his shirt front.

'That bunch of crooks,' scoffed Greg. 'They'd cut your throat and dump you in the sea tomorrow. You seriously trust them?'

'They've been good to me, boy,' Dorrell told him. 'Do you know how big these guys are?'

The radio set crackled. Dorrell didn't seem to hear it. It was mounted on a bracket at the rear of the wheelhouse. There was a hiss of static. And then, Tom's voice came through as clear as a bell. For a second, Greg was dumbfounded. Then he was yelling, 'Tom! Tom! It's me. Greg! Get help!'

'Shut your gob!' ordered Dorrell and lurched towards the set.

As he fumbled with the microphone, Greg shouted at the top of his voice, 'Tell Dad I'm on a boat in the Sound. Get the police.'

Dorrell had his back to him and was speaking into the set. He stood there calling and calling but not getting any response. He threw the microphone down and stalked towards Greg.

'Trying to get me into trouble, were you? Didn't work did it? It's a two-way set so your mate couldn't hear you.' He drew his fist back menacingly. 'You little creep. After all I've done for you! I'll stick one on you with pleasure, mate.'

The other boat was only a hundred yards off their bow! Greg didn't dare look at Dorrell in case the excitement showed on his face. It must be heading for them. It had to be. If he could just stop Dorrell looking behind him . . .

'So what's a mega scientist like you doing with this bunch of crooks?' Greg demanded sarcastically. 'They're about as dumb as rabbits themselves.'

Dorrell kicked him on the shins. 'You're just a stupid kid. You know that?' he shouted. He drained the bottle and pitched it over the side. 'Those rabbits are worth millions. Millions!' The man's sour breath filled Greg's nostrils. 'And all thanks to me.'

He made a grab at Greg's hair. Greg yelled in fury and brought his knee up smartly. It caught Dorrell high on the side of his leg. He cursed and backed off, holding the place with both hands.

Wildly, Greg looked round. There was no sign of the other boat. It must have sheered away at the last moment. He screamed at the unfairness of it all. He had been so sure.

Now Dorrell was shouting at him. 'I'll kill you for that. I'll bloody kill you!' He lurched across and threw a punch into Greg's face. Greg tried to ward it off but his arm felt like lead. Dorrell's fist caught him on the ear. He flinched away and saw a man swing himself up on to the deck. There was another fisherman close behind.

Dorrell grabbed him by the throat and bunched his fist. Then a strong arm whipped round his neck and the next moment he was sprawled across the deck, retching noisily. The boat was full of people shouting and chattering in a language Greg couldn't understand. Dazed, he shook his head, hardly able to believe what was happening.

'Nice boat you got here, skipper,' said Sam,

grinning at him. 'Fancy a new crew?' He stooped
and cut the rope.

Thirty-four

Sarah Bradley was not in a good mood. Her horse
had reared and thrown her. Now her shoulder was
bruised and painful. The horse had stepped on a
wasp's nest and bolted. She had been five miles
from Balgarri when it had happened. It had taken
her half an hour to recapture the animal. During
the ride back home she could feel the bruising
beginning to spread.

She went to the first-aid box then into the kitchen
to make a sandwich and a large cup of black coffee.
The telephone answering machine was bleeping.
There was only one message on it. She assumed it
was Bob telling her he had landed safely. But it
wasn't.

It was the duty nurse in the Flying Doctor's office

asking if she could come in next Friday. Sarah called her back. She thought the woman sounded hesitant, almost as if she was embarrassed.

'Is there anything else?' Sarah prompted.

The woman gave a self-conscious little laugh. 'Well . . .' she began. 'It's just that I got a very strange call this morning. From a boy called Tom . . .'

'Tom!' Sarah's jaw dropped in surprise. 'Did you say Tom?'

'That's your nephew's name, isn't it? The one who's staying with you? This one sounded English too.'

Sarah sat down heavily. 'You'd better tell me exactly what he said.'

Thirty-five

Bob Bradley eased the joystick forward and watched the tarmac rise to meet him. He was sorry to be taking the helicopter back. He loved flying. He glanced up and watched the rotor blades flick to a sudden stop. Another cattle muster over. Another year gone. How time flew. Still, he reflected, it wasn't all bad. He'd be spending the night with Jim MacIntyre and his family. And that was definitely something to look forward to.

Inside the small terminal, he handed the ignition key back. 'There's an urgent message for you, Mr Bradley,' the receptionist told him, handing him a slip of paper. He found a telephone.

'Hi there!' he called. 'What's up?'

He listened with rising incredulity. 'But there was

no problem when Greg called in last night,' he protested. 'You sure you got this right? It's not some sort of joke?'

'OK! OK!' he spluttered a few moments later. 'I'm sorry!' His mind raced. 'Listen! I'll take the 'copter back up and head for the river and this research place. I'll need to refuel first so it'll take an hour to get there. Call MacIntyre right away. Tell him to put out a full police alert!'

He slammed the phone down and ran as fast as he could back to reception.

Thirty-six

'I was parked just there,' Danny shouted pointing at the bushes. 'The kid was inside. Sitting in this same damn seat. When he saw me he ran for it.'

'Where'd he go?' Coyle questioned.

Danny waved an arm. 'Over there somewhere. Into the bush. I couldn't keep up with him.'

Coyle shrugged. 'Well . . . let's hope a snake gets him. Hey! Look at that,' he chuckled. Merv did a great job on those kids' 4×4. That won't start for months!'

A thought struck Danny. He yanked at the handbrake and ran down to the dinghy. 'It's fine,' he called a couple of minutes later. 'No one's touched it.'

Coyle looked at the dinghy and grunted. 'I hate

going in this thing,' he confided. 'Always felt the bottom was going to drop out or something.'

Danny laughed. 'This'll be the last time for both of us,' he said cheerfully. 'So you don't have to worry for much longer.'

He held the dinghy steady while Coyle clambered in. Danny shot a quick glance along the river then bent over the engine. The outboard tried to start, coughed and then stalled. Danny muttered to himself and pressed the starter again. The engine spluttered a few more times and cut out again.

'What's wrong with it?' Coyle complained. He got to his feet. The dinghy rocked.

'There's a blockage,' Danny shouted back. 'And sit down or you'll have us both in the water. You want that?'

Coyle sat down. He looked round and shivered. Everything seemed to have suddenly gone very still. The birds were silent. And the sun didn't feel as hot as usual. It seemed as if an invisible mist had seeped in between themselves and the rest of the world. Or was it all his imagination? This place had always given him the creeps.

'It's weed,' said Danny peering down into the river. 'That damn bootlace stuff. It's all wrapped round the prop shaft. I'll have to go overboard to clear it.'

'Well hurry it up then!' Coyle snapped.

Danny glared at him. A pulse high up on his temple began to throb. He took a deep breath and ducked down below the surface. The water felt cold. The weed was as thick as a man's thumb. It took a little while to cut it free. The weed was tough and rubbery and his knife kept slipping. He hacked and tugged with his fingers dislodging the weed a couple of centimetres at a time.

'So how much longer?' Coyle grumbled when Danny next came up for breath. He looked at his watch. 'I don't like leaving Dorrell on his own for too long. Come on Danny. Hurry it up for pete's sake!'

Danny hung on to the stern, wiping water from his eyes. At that moment he could have killed Coyle. 'Just keep a good lookout,' he warned and disappeared again. A bird screamed and the sound tore through the stillness.

The next time he came up he threw a piece of weed at Coyle. 'All done,' he called, hauling himself back in the dinghy. 'Please let it start this time,' he prayed. He jabbed the button and the engine roared into life. A small cloud of blue exhaust clung to the stern.

'Sit tight!' he shouted and gunned the throttle hard. He breathed a heartfelt sigh of relief as the bows lifted and the boat gathered speed.

Three hundred metres downstream, Kyrek lay motionless on his favourite sandbank basking in the sun. A white egret perched on his half-open jaws cleaning out the putrid matter from between his teeth. Kyrek's eyes were closed and he looked fast asleep. But while the bird bobbed and pecked, Kyrek was seething with anger.

The small, silver-coloured challenger had returned. It roared defiance at him earlier that day but refused to stop and fight. Kyrek had tried to catch it but it had got away again. It was faster than him.

Other animals would have seen it happening. Information would spread along the river that he was not as fast as he had been. More rival challengers would come, smaller crocodiles unworthy of his attention. But they could tire him before he met the next serious contender for his territory.

Kyrek ground his teeth. The bird hopped out just in time and scolded the crocodile. Then it stood beside the massive jaws and began to preen itself. Suddenly Kyrek's eyes flicked open. The intruder was coming back! For the third time that morning, he heard the sound of the engine.

With a bellow of rage, Kyrek raced through the shallows and slid down into the river.

Thirty-seven

'So let's step on the gas,' Coyle grumbled, looking at his watch.

'Don't worry. We'll be at the *Bluewater* in an hour,' Danny called.

Coyle nodded and sketched a smile. They were moving quickly now and he enjoyed the rush of air on his face.

Danny glanced over his shoulder. The wake bubbled deep and straight. No problems with the prop and the engine was running sweetly. He watched the wash breaking along the river bank behind them and heaved another sigh of relief. It should be plain sailing from now on. He just had to get them to the fishing boat.

Coyle sat facing him. 'What about the boy?' Coyle

shouted above the noise of the engine.

Danny shrugged. 'Your decision,' he called. He was busy looking out over the upraised bows at the river ahead. 'Either you let him go or . . . you don't.'

Coyle scowled. 'I'm worried what that fool Dorrell might have told him,' he confided.

Danny made a face and looked over Coyle's shoulder. There was something in the river ahead of them. A tree trunk by the look of it. He pushed the rudder over a little to take them clear of it. Then he turned his attention back to Coyle.

'So get rid of him. What's the problem?' he called back.

Fifty metres away, Kyrek raised his head high out of the water and brought it smashing down with a crack like a field gun. Then he slid his huge bulk beneath the surface and in one great, twisting surge of power, spun round and headed for the intruder.

'What the heck was that?' demanded Coyle, turning round.

Danny shrugged. He indicated the engine and shook his head. Coyle really was uptight today. Danny peered ahead, wondering where the log had got to. Frowning, he began to stand up to see better.

There was a tremendous crash! The bows reared

up. Coyle yelled in fright, lost his balance and fell backwards. His weight saved them. For a split second the dinghy hung almost vertically then fell back into the river in a sheet of spray.

Danny wrenched at the throttle and cut the scream of the engine as the dinghy rocked wildly. Water poured in over the sides. 'Christ! We're sinking!' Coyle shrieked. 'We're sinking!'

'Sit down! Sit down!' Danny screamed. 'Or you'll have us over!' He grabbed the rudder, throttled the speed right back and the wild see-sawing motion began to ease.

There was blood in Danny's mouth. He must have bitten his tongue but he couldn't remember when. He spat out the blood and crouched in the stern to get his wits back.

His calmness reassured Coyle who stopped his hysterical screaming. He began to curse instead.

'What was it?' he yelled. 'You hit a rock or something? Thought you said you knew all about boats. Jeez! Some sailorman, I don't think.'

Danny shook his head. 'Must have been that tree trunk.'

'Some tree trunk,' Coyle trumpeted. 'More like the Rock of Gibraltar,' he added sarcastically.

'Do something useful will you!' an infuriated Danny shouted back. 'Try bailing us out. Use your shoe or your hat.' He throttled back even further. There was no point putting any additional strain on the hull.

Thirty metres behind them, Kyrek surfaced. Coyle would have seen him if he had not been bending down. He came in fast.

Some sixth sense warned Danny. He spun round leaving Coyle's shout behind him in the boat. He saw a head, a nightmare head with jagged teeth coming to claim him. He screamed and jerked the tiller hard over.

Danny caught a gush of foul breath from the crocodile's jaws as it battered into the stern. The engine raced, drowning Coyle's screams. There was a loud grating sound and the dinghy shuddered. Then a trail of bubbles sped away under the boat and disappeared into the depths.

Thirty-eight

A minute passed. Then another. The two men stared at each other, faces rigid with terror. Unable to move. Convinced if they did that the monster would return. More time ticked by. A butterfly fluttered round their heads. It settled on Coyle's arm and stayed there opening and closing its wings. Then it flew away.

Coyle swallowed the bile in the back of his throat. He took a deep breath then several more. He forced himself to look at the river. He looked back over his shoulder and then past Danny. He took another deep breath and slowly leant towards him.

'It's gone Danny! It's gone!' he whispered.

Danny burst into tears. Coyle let him cry for a while. 'We were lucky. My God . . . we were lucky!'

He leant over and slapped Danny gently across the face. 'Start her up,' he encouraged. 'I need to know if it still works.'

Shaking with fear, Danny turned his head and looked over the stern. 'The prop shaft's bent,' he mumbled, 'and the engine bracket's almost off. It won't hold much longer.'

Coyle put his hands on his knees. 'So this is what we do my friend. We'll head for the shore. Find the Land Rover and drive round to *Bluewater*. We'll hire a local boat out to her.' Danny nodded. He was not shaking quite as much. 'All right then! Start her up,' Coyle encouraged. 'Let's get the hell out of here!'

The engine fired first time. With a final frightened look round, Danny pushed the rudder over and in a few seconds they were heading towards the river bank. Coyle looked up at the sky and shouted, 'Thank you God!' at the very top of his voice. He grinned at Danny and raised both thumbs.

Danny nodded and even managed a weak smile. It didn't last long. Coyle saw his mouth distort in a silent scream and knew exactly what he was looking at. There was a loud splash and the terrible head reared up alongside, close enough to touch. Kyrek looked at the men shrinking away from him and his eyes glowed.

He bit down savagely into the side of the boat. He wrenched his head from side to side. His teeth sliced through the metal as if it had been cooking foil. And all the time his eyes never left the men huddling together in the stern.

Deliberately, he began to clamber in through the jagged hole he had made. The dinghy tipped over. Danny and Coyle screamed and hung on frantically to stop themselves sliding down towards those jaws.

Kyrek's breath was warm and fetid. It was the stench of the grave itself. He eased his body further into the boat and looked at them. A silence fell. But this was no ordinary silence. It was the paralysing horror that shocks even men like Coyle and Danny into total paralysis.

They were looking at the most unspeakable death of all. Tears ran down their faces. Kyrek was no ruthless gunman they could plead with. No mother's son with a shared common humanity. He was a monster who would chew their soft human bodies with the same disregard as if they had been a dog or a wild goat. And there was no escape for either of them.

Kyrek made a sudden lunge. He seized Coyle by the left leg, just above the knee and pulled him out of the boat. It was a gentle movement rather like someone plucking an overripe fruit from the branch of a tree. Coyle tottered, windmilling his arms to keep his balance and fell across the crocodile's snout. He lay there in an obscene embrace as they disappeared under the surface.

The dinghy turned over trapping Danny inside. He had known fear in his life many times before but never anything like this. There was a sudden convulsive upheaval in the water below him. Danny was buoyed up by a great surge of water and tossed clear. Mad with terror he kicked out. There was a jar as his foot hit something very hard.

It was Kyrek swimming fast, disorientated and half-blinded by the still-racing propeller which had ripped through the skin at the corner of his eye. Blood poured out of the wound staining the river. Kyrek writhed in shock and pain, his jaws opening and closing as the huge muscles inside his body contracted rapidly in distress.

Thirty-nine

Coyle groaned in agony. The throb of pain from his leg was dreadful. He tried to shout but nothing happened. Just a dry croaking. He opened his eyes and found Danny stooping over him. Danny said nothing. He lifted Coyle under the shoulders and went on dragging him away. The jolting made the pain even worse.

They were on a wide sandbank. In front of them, the river flowed peacefully. A small fish rose to snatch an insect and sank back leaving a spreading circle of ripples. There was a loud buzzing from somewhere nearby and it took Coyle a little while to focus on the cloud of blowflies following them.

Danny dragged him slowly up the river bank and then after many stops towards the open ground beyond. Eventually they got there and Danny sank down on to the ground and slept for fifteen minutes with his head on Coyle's chest. Slowly, Coyle became fully conscious. When he couldn't bear the weight of the man's head on him any more, he made a superhuman effort and sat upright. He shook Danny awake.

They made better progress now. Coyle used his good leg to push himself along. The other trailed in the dust and new swarms of flies fell greedily on the drips left in its track. They stopped at a tree with low spreading branches.

'Eric . . . listen to me,' Danny said urgently. 'Eric I'm going to leave you here while I go and get help. You'll be safe I promise. I'll come back. I swear it on my mother's grave. I'll come back for you.'

Coyle nodded. The pain was not as sharp as it had been. It was more of a dull ache. It was thirst that now troubled him the most. Between them, they propped him in the fork of the tree, his damaged leg dangling beneath him.

'You'll be OK,' Danny reassured him. 'I'll be back. Don't worry. Sleep all you can.' Then he turned and walked away and Coyle quickly lost sight of him.

The sun beat down remorselessly. Coyle's eyelids

flickered then closed. He woke up with a start and clutched at the tree to steady himself. The heat was like an oven drying the life out of him. His tongue was swollen. It seemed to fill his mouth.

Where was Danny? Danny had gone for help! Coyle checked his watch trying to remember how long the man had been gone for. The watch was heavy and made of gold. He looked down at his leg and gave a shudder of revulsion. It was black with flies and enormously swollen. Pieces of shinbone pierced the skin.

He took a fresh grip on the branch and looked around. He wondered what had woken him. On the far side of the clearing, a bush shook. He saw the shiver running through its dry branches. Now the one in front was also beginning to shake. It dawned on him. Someone was coming. Danny! It was Danny! Good old Danny!

He tried to cheer but his throat was too dry. But the feeling of relief and happiness brought tears to his eyes. It was going to be all right after all. It was fantastic. Then he had a sudden terror that he might walk past and not see him. His excitement turned to panic. He wanted to shout 'Over here!' but the words would not come. He banged his good foot against the tree. In an agony of apprehension, he followed the moving bushes. Yes! They were coming towards him. He began to smile.

And then he saw the crocodile standing there, its snout lifting towards him where he sat helpless. Coyle roared and begged God to save him. Then the ground rose to meet him and he was dragged away.

There was a rushing noise overhead. It was getting very loud. Great billows of sand swirled round him. He could hardly breathe. But Kyrek walked steadily on.

Overhead, the helicopter hovered as low as it dared, trying to head the crocodile off. The scrub grew thicker as they neared the water, forcing the machine to go higher. On board, Bob Bradley watched in horror as the crocodile dragged the man into the river.

It spun the body over its head and fell on top of it. There was a huge splash followed later by two bursting bubbles of air. The helicopter lurched upwards and sped away. The fierce down draught subsided and the ripples faded. Peace slowly returned to the river.

Forty

Tom was lost. He had no idea where the river was. The scrub was thick here. He couldn't see more than twenty metres in front of him. For all he knew, the river might be only fifty metres away. But he could also be walking away from it into the middle of nowhere. He had to find it! The river was his lifeline back to the rest of the world.

It was getting hotter and he had no water with him. He fought down a surge of panic. He had to think clearly. His life depended upon it. He tried desperately to remember what Sam had told him to do if this ever happened.

There was a stick lying on the ground in front of him. Yes! He remembered now. And it all came back to him. He knelt down and pushed the stick into the sand. He scratched a mark with his finger at the far end of the shadow and waited. He could hear Sam's voice telling him what to do.

He counted up to three hundred and did the same again. The shadow had lengthened. Not much but enough to measure. He had found where north was. Brilliant! He visualised the map and knew the river must also be north of here. He began to walk counting his paces out loud. It wasn't easy keeping in a straight line but he did the best he could.

Forty minutes later, when he was really starting to worry, he stumbled out on to the river bank. It was a wonderful feeling. Below him, the water sparkled and his thirst was suddenly irresistible.

He reached down and scooped up a handful of water. Nothing happened. His heart raced. He looked all around then closed his eyes and dipped his head under the surface. He drank for ten long seconds until fear got the better of him. The next moment he was racing back into the scrub. When he had got his breath back, he turned and faced west. This was the direction he had come from to get away from Danny.

He broke into a steady trot searching ahead for the drowned 4×4. A snake wriggled across his path but was gone in a flash. He ran past a huge termite mound, around a clump of thorn trees and there was their 4×4 half submerged in the river. Parked nearby was the men's Land Rover. He had made it! He shouted in delight and ran forward.

A man came round the back of the Land Rover. A wild-looking man with torn clothes and a misshapen ear. Tom skidded to a halt. He tried to turn, slipped and fell over. Terrified, he looked up at the man. Who ignored him! Instead, he began to pace up and down talking and arguing with himself.

Open-mouthed, Tom stared at him. The man was less than two metres away. Suddenly, Danny swung round and pointed at him. 'You got the key?' he demanded banging the Land Rover door with his fist. Tom shook his head helplessly.

Danny groaned. 'I've lost it. And Coyle's waiting for me to come back. He can't walk. He's losing blood fast. He's a mess.'

There was a buzzing sound in the distance. 'Where's Greg?' Tom shouted. 'What have you done with him?'

Danny ignored him. He opened the door and rummaged inside. He emerged holding a packet of cigarettes and a silver lighter. Tom saw his hands shaking. Danny flicked the lighter. A streak of flame shot up towards his face. He dropped the lighter with a yell. The flame vanished.

'Why can't that man walk?' demanded Tom.

'Ever heard of crocodiles?' Danny screamed at him. 'It attacked us!' He slumped down beside the front wheel and began sobbing hysterically. The buzzing was much louder now.

'It's a helicopter!' Tom yelled, cursing himself for not realizing it sooner. 'It's the police! Look! Here it comes!'

He started to dance and whoop and wave his arms over his head. The helicopter was about a mile away and closing rapidly. But as they watched, it began to turn away. Tom could see its silhouette changing. It dipped steeply towards the river and disappeared from sight behind a tall row of trees.

'He's going!' Danny screamed. 'Stop him!'

'How? What with?' Tom shouted in confusion. He saw the cigarette lighter glinting in the sun. A flare! There were some in the vehicle. Beside the back door. Sarah had told him about them.

'Come on!' he shouted at Danny and raced down to the river. He pulled himself up on to the rear bumper and tugged at the door handle. Nothing happened. He pulled again, this time with all his strength. It moved a couple of centimetres but that was all. He fell back into the water with a splash.

The angle of the vehicle and the weight of the spare wheel were too much. He'd never get it open on his own. Where was Danny? There was no sign of him. He listened. The noise of the helicopter was fading.

Frantically, Tom waded round to the open passenger door. Inside, the water reached the bottom of the windscreen. He clambered over the front seat, caught his foot and fell full length into a sodden mess of cardboard and plastic bags.

But he had spotted the red flare box. It was still safely out of the water. He held it high over his head as he splashed his way back. The helicopter was on the move again. It gave a loud roar and he knew it was climbing.

Danny was pointing at the sky and screaming at him to hurry. Tom pulled out a flare. It was like a huge firework. He tried to read the instructions but the words were a meaningless jumble. The engine note was changing. He looked up. It was turning away. Its nose was dipping down. In a few more seconds it would be racing away.

Tom ripped off the safety band. He held the flare at arm's length. There was a loud bang. The smell of cordite and a long trail of bright red smoke went whooshing up into the clear blue sky.

Forty-one

'They were lucky!' Sergeant MacIntyre told Bob Bradley. 'Very lucky. In fact,' he went on gravely, 'they'll never know how lucky they were.'

'Big-time crooks then?' asked Bob.

MacIntyre nodded. 'Premier league. According to Dorrell, who's singing like a bird, it was one of the really big South American drug cartels. Coyle was their number one guy in Australia. Danny was his hatchet man.'

'You know what Greg told us Dorrell said on the boat,' said Bob quietly. 'Is all that true?'

MacIntyre nodded. 'What a waste of a life. Dorrell was a brilliant chemist. He was doing a lot of pure research in those days. He discovered how to make this stuff that produced a fantastic reaction in humans.'

Bob interrupted. 'What sort of reaction?'

'The ultimate performance-enhancing drug,' the policeman told him. 'He called it rocket fuel and tried to contact one of the big cartels.'

Bob frowned. 'You mean he looked them up in the phone book or something?'

MacIntyre shook his head. 'He told a pusher on the campus. It took eight months more while they checked him out before anyone came to see him.'

'What happened then?'

MacIntyre spread his hands. 'They were impressed. This country's stiff with rabbits so they set the operation up here. They registered it as a legitimate research business. Then because the drug's so powerful, they could ship the stuff out in small regular consignments which no one ever noticed. Clever.'

'So why were they closing the place down?' Bob asked, puzzled.

'According to Dorrell,' Sergeant MacIntyre told him, 'a rival organization was about to muscle in. His masters couldn't risk Dorrell falling into their hands. It would all have worked if we hadn't disturbed them.'

Bob shook his head. 'Nothing to do with us! You mean Greg and Tom and Sam Minamurra.'

MacIntyre nodded and smiled. 'You're right. It was all thanks to them. They deserve a medal but ... there'll be no publicity. It could put their lives back in jeopardy again. What's happening to them, by the way?'

Bob looked at his watch and stood up. 'This afternoon I'm driving everyone up for a corroboree at Sam's village. It's Tom's last night. And from what I hear, it's going to be quite a thrash!'

Forty-two

'Just listen to that!' Bob exclaimed some hours later.

'What is it? What's making that booming noise?' Tom demanded.

'It's the didgeridoos,' Greg told him. 'They're warming up.'

Tom stopped in disbelief. 'It's the what?'

'Didgeridoos! They're long, hollowed-out logs,' Sarah told him. 'They blow through them. You'll see. Oh look! Here's Sam.'

'We've got a big surprise for you!' Sam whispered to Tom as he led them along the sand to the ceremonial ground under the palm trees.

The sun was setting and the first stars of the evening were appearing as they were shown to their places. To the west, out over the sea, the horizon was ablaze. They were brought coconuts to drink from. Looking around, Sarah thought there must be at least two hundred people squatting in a wide circle between the palm trees.

'This is going to be quite a show,' Bob murmured. 'They must have come from all round the coast to be here for this.'

The musicians were grouped together. They clashed boomerangs together or drummed on flat pieces of wood which made a hollow, wobbling sound. Two large fires crackled and flared in the growing darkness. The smoke had a sweet scent to it. And all the time the steady grumble of the didgeridoos sawed away at their senses.

The audience gave a sigh of appreciation and started to slap their thighs. An old man with white wrinkled hair began to chant. Everyone took it up. Soon, they started to sway. Then with a loud shout, a band of fiercely-painted warriors burst out of the darkness and ran screaming into the middle of the clearing.

Their faces and chests were plastered with white mud. Their hair was braided and spiked. There were thick bunches of leaves tied around their ankles. They brandished short stabbing spears and ran forward, jabbing at the audience. They formed a swaying line, ducking and weaving only a couple of feet away from where Tom sat, enthralled.

The warriors began to stamp their feet. The audience roared encouragement and the ground trembled. The noise from the didgeridoos was overwhelming. Now the watchers were on their feet, stamping and clapping. The emotion seized hold of them all and Tom danced with an abandon he had never thought possible.

When at last it was over, they gathered in groups around leaf mats heaped with food. Sam squatted beside Tom. Neither of them spoke much. There was no need to. After they had eaten, Winyara walked out into the middle of the dancing ground and put up his hand. He spoke for a long time.

Sam suddenly took hold of Tom's arm and brought him to his feet. People were smiling and shouting encouragement. The band waved their boomerangs and blew a single massive blast on the didgeridoos. And Tom Woods, schoolboy, found himself walking into the centre of everyone's attention.

He stood beside Sam in a daze. The noise of the audience merging now with the roar of the incoming tide. Shadows from the fire slanted across the sand. Sam's voice was hoarse and Tom saw he was pouring with sweat. As if in a dream, he felt Sam embrace him and take a garland from two women and place it over his head.

Then he held out his hand, European-style, and grinned at Tom. 'Bad news for you,' he called. 'You're my brother now!' And Tom hugged him. The music and dancing resumed in earnest and not long afterwards, Bob and Sarah took them back to their sleeping quarters.

'Reveille at six tomorrow morning for everyone,' Bob told them. 'We've got a long day ahead of us.'

Much later, Tom woke. He lay on his back gazing at the stars and marvelling at their size and brightness. The music formed the perfect backdrop to the last few hours he had remaining in this magical country.

Greg's voice beside him gave him a start. 'Been meaning to tell you . . .' Greg said sleepily. There was a long silence and Tom thought he must have dozed off. Greg yawned. 'You did well. I'm glad you're Sam's brother,' he muttered. 'Sorry you've got to go back. You'd make a good Aussie!' Then he turned over and went to sleep.

The drums became more insistent. They seemed to be calling him and a little later, unable to resist, Tom slipped out of his blankets and made his way back to the leaping firelight. The dancers opened their ranks and welcomed him inside.

Heathrow was grey, wet and bustling. 'You've got a good tan,' his father said, pushing the luggage trolley.

'We got your postcard,' his mother told him.

'Yes! Why didn't you write more?' his father questioned. 'You had enough time. Your mother was quite upset.'

'You did promise,' she reminded him.

Tom opened his mouth to explain then shut it again.

'And what's all this about you helping the police?' his father wanted to know.

'I hope you weren't being a nuisance,' his mother added.

They put his case in the boot of the old Renault. Tom noticed that the back light was still broken. 'The neighbour's cat was run over yesterday,' his mother told him.

When they eventually got out on to the motorway,

210

his father looked in the driving mirror and asked, 'Well . . . anyway . . . did you enjoy it?'

Tom didn't reply at first. He couldn't. Instead he felt a wave of longing break inside him. He swallowed. His eyes were suddenly burning. 'Yes,' he said after a long pause. 'Yes, it was great!'

Postscript

It was night. A warm humid night. A foretaste of the rains that would soon sweep in from the ocean. The air was heavy with scents and the night animals were busy.

A bush mouse stopped its scurrying to listen for enemies. It sat up on its haunches, head to one side, whiskers quivering in concentration. Reassured, it relaxed and began grooming itself. Half a metre away, a brown snake silently coiled itself into a powerful spring and measured the distance of its strike.

Kyrek was lying motionless on the bank listening to the night. His damaged eye was slowly getting better. He was not hungry. Four metres below him, the hull of a silvery-coloured boat lay upside down on the river bed. It was now the home of shoals of small fish who fought fierce silent battles to protect their new empire from all rivals.

A man's gold watch lay beside it, half buried in the sand. It still kept excellent time. There was no moon. High above in the immensity of the heavens, a tiny light flashed. In time, it vanished and only then did the noise of the four jet engines reach the river. But it was a faint sound like that of very distant thunder.

Kyrek listened and discarded it. In the thorn tree opposite, the butcher bird slept and dreamt of what it would catch and impale there the next day. Kyrek eased forward and sank to the bottom of the river. He would wait for the sun to rise and warm him.

BRUNNER

Geoffrey Malone

Brunner's family is killed by hunters. He flees across the snowy wilderness to find a new home with the beavers of Lake Napachokee.

But nowhere is safe from humans. Greedy developers begin bulldozing and dynamiting the lakeshore to build a holiday resort. For Brunner it's a desperate struggle to save them all from destruction.

TORN EAR

Geoffrey Malone

The wind carried the scent of blood far into the night, while the vixen still pawed at the broken little bodies on the pile of earth . . .

But Torn Ear survives the gamekeeper's attack. Slowly his mother introduces him to the fox's world – the skills of hunting and how to avoid danger. Then he is on his own.

Until he meets Velvet, and they have their own cubs. But man intervenes again, and his favourite cub is threatened. Torn Ear must rescue her, but will he escape the clutches of the gamekeeper this time?

KIMBA

Geoffrey Malone

Kimba was born among the boulders on M'goma Hill in the scorching heat of the afternoon.

Nurtured by his mother, fierce, tender Sabba, he learns the ways of the plains – the merciless hunt for food, the dangers from ravenous hyenas, leopards, snakes, crocodiles – and rival lions.

But when strange lions challenge his father, Blank Mane, for leadership of the pride, Kimba is running for his life . . .

ELEPHANT BEN

Geoffrey Malone

Ben is travelling in the African Plains with his game ranger father. It's a chance he's longed for, to really see the animals in the wild.

This territory is roamed by the great elephant Temba and her family in their daily hunt for food, their battles against ravenous lions and crocodile who prey on young elephant calves.

But, unknown to Ben, other humans are near. And their interests in the elephants is very different. For Temba and her family – a terrifying battle for survival . . . and for Ben.